The Pinocchio Project

Book 3 of the Mari Fable Mysteries

Emily Fluke

Also by Emily Fluke

"To all the moms who reach out and help other moms. You're the real heroes.
It takes a village."

Author's Note

Please be aware that this book deals with the sensitive topic and theme of infertility.

Prologue

Dear Journal,

A month ago, I met Pinocchio. At least, I assume it's Pinocchio. Except his name is Carlo. It wasn't until we spent more time together that I noticed he obsessively scratched at his skin. I'm no doctor, but it didn't look healthy. I chalked it up to nerves when he'd spoken about the anonymous company's plan to buy out his game, but I can't ignore the obvious—he's turning into a puppet.

I wrote an article about the gaming company, as promised (plus, it was an excuse to research the place I swear Johnson was hiding). Unfortunately, the article was pulled from all sources, and all the news about Carlo vanished. How the company had virtually erased Carlo's footprint on the internet, I have no clue. Such a feat would take god-level Googling.

I worry about Carlo, and I want to find Johnson, but this will be a long road to trek. Unfortunately (x2), I have other fairy tales to take care of, a job to do at Bay Side Media (not to mention a new nutty intern to train), and a daughter to raise.

Cinderella appeared in San Francisco, and Mr. Darcy still needs my help to find Elizabeth. For now, I have Scarlet and Kai's help with research on Carlo and Johnson and the game. So far, we've only learned that Carlo's claim about simulated bodies didn't work—at least not for most players. I'll continue to ask Mr. Geppetto about Pinocchio/Carlo but I don't have a picture to show him and Mr. G doesn't have the story aura. So that's a bust.

This entry is brief because Scarlet is supposed to meet me at Pioneer Park where we'll trade, teaching each other new skills. She'll practice taking notes about a fake crime scene while I'll try to create portals for the first time.

Wish me luck. Scar is a terrible teacher and I really, <u>really</u> don't want to fail.

Chapter 1

Facing the Music

(2 years and 2 months later)

Why didn't moms get lollipops for surviving a terrifying experience, AKA the first day of preschool? Wendy bounded ahead of me, yanking on my arm with her sweaty hand wrapped in mine. She didn't give two Pull-Ups about growing up too fast. But I did. I needed the sugar rush from a cherry-flavored sucker to keep my baby-is-too-big tears at bay. My crying could probably fill up the San Francisco Bay after today.

I'd jump in the bay for a crisp, icy swim to clear my head, except I'd probably just run into the Little Mermaid. And I didn't have the emotional capacity to tell the poor girl that her entire existence would be torture as per the original fairy tale—unless we discovered a way to twist the story, of course.

Instead of seawater, I tasted the salt from the sweat that clung to the peach fuzz on my upper lip. *Note to self: schedule a wax appointment before finding the crazy guy who disappeared into a pixilated tree after trying to steal my clothes.* Okay, clothes equaled an invisible Red Riding Hood cloak, and the pixilated world inside a tree was more like…Nope, wait, that was accurate.

Still, fighting Frankenstein's monster, watching my mother fly away as a swan, and even cutting myself out of the wolf's stomach paled compared to leaving Wendy behind.

The waxy smell of crayons filled the school hallway. Reality was worse than any story I could imagine. Wendy pulled free from my grasp and skipped toward the open door.

"Wait for mommy," I managed with a voice cracking as much as our SUV's windshield after Scarlet practiced driving for the first time and crashed into a lamppost.

Wendy didn't even glance back as she skipped along with bouncing pigtails. I swore the sweat on my lip doubled. I hurried ahead and held out my hand again. Joy flooded me as my daughter wrapped her hand in mine. When would I be ready for my baby to grow up? Maybe when she turned forty. The half-pint, pear-shaped teacher with yellowing highlights smiled as bright as her hair. What if she was a monster hiding in plain sight? Miss Jenna could be Maleficent—no, the witch from Hansel and Gretel! I squinted at the doorway into the classroom to spy for something resembling an oven.

Kai's voice repeated in my head. He'd insisted I used fairy tales to hide behind when really this was me refusing to accept my mommy's girl had reached school age.

Black spots dotted my vision, and I forced myself to take a deep breath. The tightness in my chest and squeeze in my throat didn't make for a cleansing inhale.

One would think I was a magician about to perform an impossible feat in front of a live studio audience.

And one would be right.

The audience? Twenty-one paste-eating four-year-olds. The impossible feat? Letting go of Wendy's tiny hand.

Every step toward the classroom brought the walls closer to me. The hallway narrowed, closing in on us. It was a magic trick and, I, the failed magician.

"Good morning!" Miss Jenna beamed so brightly I decided if she'd come from any story, it was Lord of the Rings. The preschool teacher was a beacon—lit to call for Gondor's aid.

"Hi," I said with a nod. Wendy released my hand and darted toward a round table with neatly stacked crayons and a coloring page with circles that read *fill in the faces with how you're feeling*. "I'm feeling like a stinky diaper," I muttered.

"What was that?" Miss Beacon—Jenna—asked.

"Poop," I said, then twisted my lips into a frown. My brain had stuttered to a halt, the little engine that couldn't. All I could think about were the baby things I'd lost. I didn't miss changing diapers, but Wendy barely even cuddled anymore. "Uh, I mean—" I leaned closer to whisper and play it off like I'd meant to say that. "It's a curse word around our house. I just wanted to warn you that my daughter isn't allowed to say it."

"Of course." She nodded, yellow hair bouncing in her half-ponytail. "We have a strict no potty-mouth policy at Evil Witch Preschool."

"Excuse me? What'd you call the school?"

"Everly Woods," Jenna repeated. "Your daughter is registered with this preschool, correct?"

"Right." My turn to nod. "Yes, she's in your classroom."

She's in your classroom. Not in my arms. Not at the daycare near my office building. Wendy was her own little person now, no longer an extension of her mommy.

I sighed. I was acting ridiculous. This was fine. *If fine meant the entire building was on fire and I'm in the middle of it.*

Miss Jenna power-walked to the front of the classroom and addressed the mingling parents, who looked at their miniatures with teary eyes.

"Parents are welcome to stay for the first twenty minutes of class," she said. "Once your children finish their first coloring assignment, you'll be allowed to take the picture, and we'd ask that you quietly exit. Please say your goodbyes now and head to the back of the room. This will allow your little ones to get acquainted with the classroom while your presence is nearby. The gentle exit will aid in keeping emotions in check. And I'm referring to the parent's emotions."

Her joke earned a few scattered chuckles from the moms and dads. I knelt beside Wendy's tiny pink chair and pulled her in for a hug. She absent-mindedly returned it, while never taking her eyes off the tower of crayons. The moment I let go, she reached for blue and scribbled over the circles on the paper.

"I love you more than anything," I said.

"Love you. Bye, mommy!"

Wendy didn't so much as look up from her masterpiece of blue faces. At least, the coloring accurately portrayed how I felt. She handed me the picture and reached for a blank piece of paper in the center of the table.

"Okay students," Miss Jenna said, "Now we're going to draw a picture of your family while your family moves to the back of the room."

I snuck another quick pat on Wendy's head that turned into a kiss on the cheek, that turned into a long hug.

"Remember that you're strong and smart and perfect an—"

"Mrs. Rowan."

I glanced up to see the teacher towering over me. Her tiny stature looked ominous now, with her hands on her hips and an air of authority. I could have sworn I was Alice, and this was Wonderland after I'd followed the "Drink Me" instructions and shrunk to a doll's size.

Miss Jenna stared down her nose at me. Did I imagine the crook in it?

Ebenezer Scrooge, she's not the witch.

I forced an awkward smile and stood. The other parents didn't mind my walk of shame to the back of the classroom. They fixed their eyes on their precious artists, scribbling the second coloring assignment of their preschool careers.

One by one the parents trailed out, leaving only me and a fidgety dad who kept telling me that this was the first time he'd be separated from his son. But even he left before I could make my feet walk out that door.

Wendy would never be my baby again and today proved that. She happily colored away, chatted about the latest Disney Junior show with her tablemates, and didn't so much as notice my presence.

I sighed and stood, finally able to head for the door without my stomach twisting so hard that it would send me to the miniature toilet in the preschool bathroom. One last look at my perfect, stinky little nugget and the color red caught my eye.

Blood cycled in my brain first. Then I realized it was crayon on the paper in front of her. Wendy was drawing the crude shape of a person —wearing a red hood.

It's me. It's a cry for her mommy!

"Mrs. Rowan," the teacher said. I leaped, my stomach in my throat now. She'd snuck up behind me, silent but deadly. I really needed to get my brain off potty-talk, but my belly twisted in all kinds of uncomfortable ways. I'd imagined the color blue when I noted my lip-waxing schedule. Now I switched to picturing brown to file the thought of checking up on my stomach issues when I got home. "Wendy is adapting to the new environment wonderfully. Now would be a good time to slip out."

"Yeah, an environment preheated to four hundred degrees," I muttered.

"Are you all right?"

I glanced at Miss Jenna and then back to Wendy. "My daughter needs me. I'll just sit quietly beside her table—"

I pushed past the teacher.

"No, Mrs. Rowan."

"You won't even notice me." I plopped down, criss-cross applesauce, behind Wendy's chair.

"It's time to leave," she said, her voice still high-pitched and bright. "Please." Wait, nope, the pitch dropped an octave lower now and a slight crease formed between her eyebrows.

"The picture she's drawing is of me, so that has to mean something."

"That is the assignment, Mrs. Rowan. You should be proud that your daughter is following instructions so well."

Like, 'climb into that oven so I can eat you?' No, thanks.

But no glow or story aura existed around Miss Jenna. That didn't mean I was ready to leave my daughter.

"Please say goodbye." She waved her hand toward Wendy.

"I'm good, thanks." I smiled.

"It's time to leave." Miss Jenna had gone from speaking in a voice so sugary it rivaled the Pop-Tarts I'd had for breakfast to talking like Batman. "Let me show you to the door." She opened her arms in the direction of the exit like Vanna White, presenting a showcase on Wheel of Fortune.

I stood but spied the bookshelf to the right. "How about I just read a quick story? Right kids?" I nodded, hoping my audience would copy the gesture.

"Uh—"

"I'm a great narrator." I snagged the closest book and skipped to the front of the room.

"Mrs. Rowan."

It was too late. I dove into the story of a girl with skin as white as snow and lips as red as blood. Of course, this rendition was all cartoons and smiling faces, which were wrong on so many levels. The book's hard cover sagged heavy in my hands. Fairy tales had a weight of their own that haunted me day and night. Kids giggled as I continued to disobey their teacher. Maybe it wasn't a great example to my daughter, but she'd appreciate story time and that was enough for me.

"Snow White falls into a deep sleep from the curse and—" I flipped the page. It showed her waking next to the prince. I snorted. "Well, it shows she lives, but Snow White definitely did not wake up. She died a tragic death and now the stepmother is an evil immortal who could terrorize the world if she wanted—"

"Mrs. Rowan!" Miss Jenna finally got the courage to cut me off. My surroundings filled in and I remembered this was a preschooler's fairy tale, not the true events of a murder investigation from years ago.

I looked up from the colorful pages to see the tiny teacher, dwarfed by the security guard, who stood next to her.

"Time to leave."

I cringed and nodded. The security guard marched to the front of the room and waved for me to lead the way before him. I walked through the maze of tables to swap the book out with another one.

"Let me try this one."

"The door Mrs. Rowan," he said.

I glanced back to see Wendy giggling over a leaning tower of crayons she'd built with the boy in the seat beside her. He knocked it down and Wendy erupted into laughter.

The long walk down the bright hallway exaggerated the distance between me and my baby with every step. The corridor seemed to stretch and expand in an arbitrary world dependent on my emotions. Sunshine flooded into the hall as the security guard opened the door and beckoned me through.

Outside, I sighed and folded my arms. The hard spine of the book dug into my ribcage. I spun around to hand it back to the security officer, but he'd already disappeared inside the door. Today, I was guilty of theft because I refused to step back into Everly Woods preschool. If I saw Wendy again, I'd run out with her, crying for her to be my baby again.

I looked down to see the book I'd grabbed. A wooden-faced boy stared back at me. I'd given up on finding Carlo, the suspected real-world Pinocchio, months ago. He could have led us to the pixilated world Johnson disappeared into, but we had no way of contacting the young man and couldn't find a trace of his existence.

What were the odds I grabbed this story? Like the glow of the aura, the hood was leading me to him.

Cars drove by on the steep San Francisco hill. The concrete jungle smelled of coffee, exhaust, and trash. One would believe it impossible for fairy tales to exist in a world like this. But one would be wrong.

I dug in my crossbody purse for my phone and tapped the group text, including my best friend and husband.

I know we've paused on Pinocchio, but even if he isn't the clue to finding Johnson; I think the hood is leading me to him.

I headed for the crosswalk and slapped my palm against the button. The signal beeped and flashed, announcing it was safe to cross. Why did The Keeper of Stories cross the street? To get to the caffeine fix on the other side. I pushed through Starbucks's doors and the delicious scent of hot bean water filled my nose.

My phone buzzed.

Scarlet: Who said I paused? You're not the boss of me.

I snorted and ordered a latte for myself and my husband. We'd taken a two-week vacation from our jobs to celebrate our anniversary, but the Keeper's responsibilities never stopped, and we both needed a buzz of energy.

Kai: You are *the boss of me. That's why I've been doing historical research on the original author of Pinocchio in secret.*

I rolled my eyes and smiled. Of course, he was—nothing stood between my husband and historical research, except my body in lingerie. I took a seat at a tall round table, the adult version of the preschooler's desks, and tapped another message.

Good, maybe we can kill two—

I backspaced. The phrase didn't sit well with me after losing my mother to her literal bird form just two years ago.

Maybe we can close Pinocchio's story and find Johnson at the same time. Carlo could lead us to that virtual reality thing.

As I leaned on the table, crumbs clung to my elbows and the sticky leftover of spilled coffee left me a mess. Blaming the rude patrons of the restaurant would get me nowhere. The mess in my life was all my own doing. Of that, I was sure.

Why did Johnson want the hood? Who *wanted* the responsibility of stopping fictional monsters from spilling into the real world? What good had I done with the hood? Fairy tales didn't always end well and twisting them risked trapping people into an immortal loop.

"Mari!"

My name had been called out a lot already today, and it was only eight in the morning. This time, it was my coffee calling. I hopped off the chair and snagged the two plastic cups of mom-fuel, then pushed out the front doors.

Everly Woods preschool was a bright building that I could see from the corner of my eye. My chest ached as if the evil stepmother had ripped my heart from my ribcage.

Motherhood was a tricky thing. Kai had suggested that my grief from saying goodbye to my mother made it harder to let Wendy go.

He was right.

But I didn't care. I marched across the street again, jay-walking since no cars approached. Maybe I could volunteer in the classroom. I'd get a helper's badge and everything. Then I wouldn't miss a second of Wendy's impossibly fast growth spurts.

My phone buzzed with a reminder, and the screen blinked. Bold letters filled the narrow screen and a small calendar appeared underneath. *Ovulation window is open!*

Saved by the fertility app. I shot a look at Everly Woods Preschool and turned away. Kai would be proud of me for giving Wendy some space—and happy that I was closing the space between us.

I tapped the app's button to check mark that I'd have sexy time today.

Chapter 2

The Face That Rings a Bell

Distant sirens of a crash piqued my ears but, unfortunately, they weren't uncommon in a city with the size and bustle of San Francisco. The real world was just as bad—no, worse—than most fairy tales. That was why I couldn't let any of the fictional monsters go rogue, further darkening the world around me.

The coffee tasted bitter now, so I tossed it into the trash and hurried home to meet up with Kai.

The temperate sixty-degree weather marked the end of summer in the Bay Area and the distant ring of a school's bell signaled the start of the school year. The higher I climbed, the easier the morning breeze could reach me, since the buildings didn't block it up here. Cool gusts tossed my short hair into my face, which left strands stuck to the nude lipstick I wore since Scarlet had watched too many makeup tutorials on YouTube and had insisted I try it.

My phone buzzed as I climbed the outdoor staircase that zigzagged up the side of our condo building. I glanced at the screen in my hand to see my husband's name on the group chat.

My parents agreed to pick up Wendy from preschool at the end of the week so we can go on our vacation! I'm not packing a single pair of underwear because we're going to be nakey-wakey-eggs-and-bakey the entire time.

"Kai!" I squealed, and tapped the message to confirm he'd sent it in the thread that included Scarlet.

Another text popped up with a GIF of Spiderman laying in bed and beckoning the viewer toward him with a flick of his finger.

Before I could stop him, Kai sent another message.

Let's start this afternoon. You + me = roleplay at The Drunken Elf. I'll be a sexy wizard coming to kidnap the sorceress' maiden.

I paused my climb, set Kai's latte down on the steps, and furiously tapped a message telling my husband to stop revealing our sex life to Scarlet.

The three dots showing an incoming message popped up before I could hit send.

Scarlet: Treat. Yo. Self. Just spare me the details next time PLEASE.

Thankfully, the former Keeper had a good sense of humor. She dealt with life in a series of TV show quotes since she took to learning about the real world through the old Boob Tube. It had become a trademark of her personality, but I wouldn't say it helped her fit in.

The phone buzzed like a bumblebee at a rave as Kai rapid-fired a thousand apology texts. I knew Scarlet well enough now to predict that she'd take this mishap as a sign from the universe (or storybook gods as she believes in), as making a mockery of her lack of love life. The poor girl just wanted a suitable date, but with her quirkiness and the amount of emotionally immature men in the city, romance didn't stand a chance.

I marched down the hall to our front door and shot a glance at my neighbor's condos. Because of his name, I'd dropped multiple hints about Pinocchio to Mr. Geppetto. The old man never took the bait, and he didn't exude the story aura, but I clung to hope that he could help us find Carlo, who'd then help us find Johnson. As an investigator, it killed me that all our leads brought us to dead-ends.

The past two years of sealing fairy tales and classic stories didn't bring many happy endings, and though it was wishful thinking, maybe

Johnson knew something about the hood and the fabric between fiction and reality that we didn't.

I unlocked the door and slipped inside to find the apartment empty. One of my many sticky notes had been torn from the block of rainbow colors and tacked to the countertop. I set the latte down and deciphered my husband's handwriting.

Treadmill on the fritz. Went for a jog in Pioneer Park.

"Hmm," I hummed, taking a sip of his coffee. It was impressive he could run and plan our vacation sexcapades at the same time. When I ran, I could focus on nothing else other than when it ended.

The house felt bare without my daughter's presence. I made for the bedroom to hunt for a dress I'd worn to the Renaissance Faire. With Kai's love of history and my recent interest in stories, we enjoyed the old-timey atmosphere. The fairs felt like a storybook I could control with no risk of danger or people dying if I failed.

The pink walls of Wendy's room caught my eye as I passed. We'd just retired her princess toddler bed for a big-girl frame with a white headboard and a twin mattress. My heart cracked a little more at the thought of the crib collecting dust in our storage unit.

I forced myself into mine and Kai's bedroom. I wanted to hurl my body onto the bed like a dramatic Disney princess, but resisted and scrounged through the closet instead. If I focused on being a sorceress and the fun week Kai and I had ahead of us, maybe I'd get my mind off the fact that I couldn't squish Wendy back down into my chubby little baby girl.

Once dressed, I flopped on the couch and dug the notebooks out from underneath the Coffe Table of Evidence. Each page was covered with sticky notes and organized by color, distinguishing from which part of the story cycle the information contained. After rereading through the puzzle pieces of evidence, I slapped the books shut, stacked them neatly on the cushion next to me and hefted myself, and the dress's heavy skirts, off the couch.

In our private text thread, Kai confirmed our meetup. To make the roleplay more believable, we agreed to arrive at the bar separately. The afternoon walk in the costume dress might draw a few eyes, but cosplay at The Drunken Elf wasn't unusual.

The smell of burgers and the wheat-heavy hint of beer blasted me as I pushed through the doors. The bar was busy for lunch with boisterous laughter, casual business meetings, and retirees scouting for a date. Some TVs streamed live Dungeons and Dragons games while others stayed more mainstream with news channels or comedy show reruns. Rachel Green from Friends laughed and grabbed Ross's arm on the TV closest to where I selected a table.

The obnoxious laugh track would definitely throw off our fantasy-style beat, so I abandoned the table and found two stools at the bar as far from the closest TV as possible. The news lady's voice still drifted into my consciousness as she spoke of Bay Area weather patterns. Science predicted more mild breezes and partially cloudy dates for the week. The weather woman ensured they'd have an update on what to expect for Labor Day weekend as the date grew closer.

Weather wasn't something I needed to worry about considering I planned to spend every second of our anniversary vacation inside a hotel room with my husband. We'd binge-eat, marathon Stranger Things, and collect a pile of lingerie laundry.

I ordered a basket of wings but skipped a cocktail in case Everly Woods preschool called with an emergency. *Wendy needs her mommy, STAT.* Truthfully, I hadn't enjoyed an alcoholic drink in over a year since I still couldn't get pregnant.

I sighed and gave up trying to ignore my sadness. Wendy looked delighted with her new friends and the coloring assignments and every pregnancy test I'd taken since we'd started trying resulted came out negative. Besides, I didn't want to be a helicopter parent. So what if I couldn't control the fairy tales as well as I'd hoped? That didn't give me permission to micromanage everything else in my life.

"Easier said than done," I mumbled into the steaming basket of buffalo sauce and chicken.

I pulled out a to-go block of Post-It notes that weighed my purse down. Worth it, considering I hated recording information on my phone and needed an on-demand notation device. If I wrote my thoughts, then threw them away, the visual could help me let go. But I didn't have the strength to accept the reality of my child growing up just yet.

Instead, I scribbled notes to organize my thoughts on the latest Keeper resolutions. I'd closed stories, but it didn't always mean a happy ending. Even when I succeeded.

In between bites of wings, I turned a napkin orange with sauce and added more cons than pros to my list of storybook cases since gaining the hood.

Orange: *Reese is steeped in depression because we haven't twisted his story yet.* The poor medical examiner struggled with the reality that he was Quasimodo in the classic tale of the Hunchback of Notre Dame. The plot meant he'd die alone, never having connected with Esmeralda, the woman of his dreams.

On the green notes: *Mom left forever, since becoming a swan. Is she happy? Will I ever know if closing that fairy tale was a good thing?*

Last but not least, I peeled a red sticky note and recorded the news of Mr. Darcy and Elizabeth's separation. *Did the story push them together when they weren't meant to be? Could I have left them alone and let their free will find them better marital partners?*

"Stupid hood," I said, as I twisted the strings of the garment around my finger.

"Who're you calling stupid?"

The stool next to me groaned as the legs dragged against the ground. Kai plopped in the seat and wiggled his eyebrows. "I'm an all-powerful wizard. Opposite of stupid." He'd managed to pull his floppy hair into a hairtie for a miniature man-bun at the crown of his head. The Viking-style look always got me hot and bothered.

The white blouse he wore framed his shoulders nicely. The sight of the shirt took me right back to baby Wendy when we'd dressed up as pirates with our daughter in a parrot costume. Tears stung my eyes.

Kai gasped and rubbed my back in little circles with his palm. "We can roleplay swashbucklers." He lowered his voice and leaned closer. "Are wizards too close to the Keeper?"

I shook my head. "It's not that." I dunked a wing in ranch dipping sauce but dropped it back in the basket, too defeated to eat. "What good have I done with the hood? Honestly?" Though thoughts of my daughter growing up sparked the emotional breakdown, I didn't want to admit it. And my failures as the Keeper were laid out in front of me in an organized pattern of sticky notes. Normally, evidence thrilled me, but a list of my wrongdoings gave me nothing but negativity—just like the pregnancy tests.

Kai's brows pinched together. He continued rubbing my back, sensing a meltdown coming. It started with Wendy growing up and would end with this stupid Keeper life.

"What do you mean? You saved your own life. You scared the Evil Queen away so she couldn't kill any more of her son's girlfriends."

"Yeah, but she *got away*." I dropped my head into my palms, then frowned, realizing I still had orange wing sauce on my fingertips. I dabbed a napkin on my hairline, but the damage was done. "Plus, I haven't figured out how to save Esmeralda and Reese from their deaths in the Hunchback. Pinocchio is missing, and Mr. Darcy and Elizabeth separated."

"Frankenstein's monster died." Kai shrugged.

I sighed. Monster or not, the death wasn't a success in my book.

"And—and, you stopped Heath and your grandmother from writing new stories and manipulating people's lives for their own immortality." My husband didn't stop there. The stool squeaked as he shifted to face me. His hands danced excitedly with his supposed proof that I wasn't a complete dumb-dumb. "What about Cinderella? You pushed that girl's story along so she wouldn't have to suffer at the hands of her drug-addicted mom. Didn't she end up marrying the CEO of that mega software company?"

I tried to smile. That story, at least, had a happy ending, and I'd helped Cinderella—or Rosa as her real name was—escape her abusive mother and find her 'prince.' It was enough to get me through the day and pull me from my funk, but I still didn't trust the hood.

I took a deep breath and started over. "Okay, sir, I don't know you. Why is your hand on my back?"

The regular bartenders at The Drunken Elf knew us by now and our odd conversations. Scarlet had earned a few embarrassing pictures on the wall of shame. When the man mixing a drink nearby heard my claim, he smirked.

"I've been sent to retrieve the woman the king has chosen to marry," Kai said after ordering a cheeseburger. "But I didn't expect you to be so captivating." He eyed my bare shoulder and traced his gaze up my neck.

"I don't think the king would like to hear you say that about his betrothed." I played along. The scenario distracted me from thinking too deeply about all the cons of the hood or Wendy's first day of school. Plus, in the roleplay world, I could control everything. The bar's buzzing lunch-hour environment helped solidify the nature of our pretend world.

A group of older women behind us cackled as a half-naked man graced the screen in a cologne commercial between the news reports.

"Oh look, there's the king," Kai joked.

I stifled a laugh. "Well, in that case, let's hurry this journey to the castle along."

My husband raised an eyebrow, not amused by the joke that I found the cologne model attractive. I didn't, but our sex life needed all the spice it could get right now. Speaking of jokes, trying to have another baby wasn't one.

No. No baby thoughts.

"So, my good man," I started. "My ovulation, or, um—our time is running out before the king arrests you for not bringing me to him." Imagination and creativity combined to enhance our playful plans. I pushed the basket of leftover wings away from me and took a sip of water.

"Right, right." He took another big bite of the burger and wiped his hands. "Let's take this food on our journey." After flagging down a server, Kai boxed up the remaining food and tucked it under his arm.

"I hope you have a horse, so we can hurry." I stood and smoothed out the ruffles on the front of my dress. Kai's post-shower smell drifted to me as he shifted on the stool to face me. I definitely wanted a piece of that.

"Oh, I have *something* for you to ride—"

Kai didn't finish his innuendo. Instead, his mouth dropped and his face paled. I snapped my neck to see the TV behind us, following my husband's gaze.

An image of a young man's face vanished before I could get a good look at it. A running commentary scrolled below the image, then switched to a live video stream from the news camera.

A reporter stood on a San Francisco street in front of a damaged car. She spoke to the cameraman. "Witnesses say the body disappeared."

"Was that—" Kai's voice trailed.

The woman gestured toward an onlooker and invited him to step into the camera's frame. "Mr. Pine caught the entire scene in the background of a video he was taking of his girlfriend's TikTok dance. What you see next will shock you."

The video filled the screen, zooming away from the girl dancing and toward the car crash in the background. A pedestrian ran onto the road. A red sedan screeched to a halt, but it was too late. The vehicle struck the man with enough force to crush every organ in his body. And it didn't stop there. The car partially tumbled over the limp body with one tire smashing the man's pelvis. The scene should have been gruesome and disturbing, with blood and limbs twisted in the wrong directions.

Instead, what happened next *did* shock me.

The man with the camera phone jogged toward the accident, keeping the stream going as he ran. Though it was blurry and moving around enough to make me motion sick, the face of the victim was undeniable.

The pointed nose, buzzed hair, and carved cheekbones made up the features of a familiar DoorDash delivery driver. One I hadn't seen in almost two years after he'd come to me for help with his video game world.

But on the screen, I couldn't see the glow of the story aura around him.

"It's Pinocchio," I said. "I mean—" But before I could call him by his real name, the body disappeared.

The car landed flat on the concrete and all traces of Carlo were gone. Gasps and screams echoed from the video.

I whipped around to stare at Kai and process what we'd just seen. The bartender stood beneath the TV.

"It's gotta be editing effects," the bartender said. "Wild, the things apps can do now." He shook his head and wiped the counter with a rag.

Kai and I remained speechless, our brains short-circuited for the moment.

The bartender kept his eyes on the ranch spill beside my basket as he wiped. "Sometimes I wonder if we're all just living in a simulation." He laughed and shook his head. "Or maybe I'm just hoping that so I don't have to deal with my crazy ex-girlfriend anymore." He cleaned up our mostly empty baskets and sauntered off.

"Now I really wish you did have a horse," I said. I picked up the heavy skirt of the Renaissance dress, and hurried for the door.

"What's your plan?" Kai knew me well enough to know the look in my eye.

"We finally have a picture of Carlo." I pointed to the phone in my hand. The video would play everywhere now. Viral status online was a gift to an investigative journalist like me when the viral content contained sensitive evidence. "It's a long shot, but we can show his face to Mr. Geppetto and see if it jogs his memory. Because of his name, he's our only connecting thread to *The Adventures of Pinocchio*."

We pushed through the double doors, and the afternoon light blinded us. My phone buzzed with the ovulation-tracking app signal that my fertility window would end soon. I tapped 'Ignore' and shoved it back into my purse.

"And Pinocchio is our only connection to Johnson." Kai threaded my train of thought together aloud.

"Exactly."

My pulse picked up. Sure, I was out of shape, but it was the excitement of having a clue that sparked the pounding in my chest. Johnson's elusiveness mocked my lack of understanding of the story cycle and all things Keeper. If I could find him, I'd get answers, and maybe better control over the stories.

We hurried across the street and down the sidewalk, rushing like two spectators about to miss the town jousting tournament.

Kai didn't so much as run out of breath, and it exaggerated the fact that I really needed to stop skipping yoga.

As we rounded the corner on Main and our condo came into view, he glanced at me. "So, does this mean no sexy time?"

Chapter 3

Let's Cut to the Chase

My plan didn't, in fact, mean no sexy time. Mr. Geppetto rarely left his house unless his girlfriend, Tala, dragged him out for coffee. Apparently, today was one of those days. While the elderly couple enjoyed their date, Kai and I enjoyed each other.

The Renaissance dress lay sprawled on the floor next to a pile of Kai's pants and pirate blouse. I rolled over, smashing my chest against the mattress, and grabbed my phone. Tala had not texted back, which wasn't unusual for her. It used to worry me to forehead sweat, but I'd grown used to it. She wasn't part of a fairy tale and hopefully would never be directly involved in one.

I swiped up to open the app. The ovulation timer dinged with a cheerful tune as I inputted the date of our intercourse. It put a clinical damper on our post-sex bliss, but I'd forget to track it if I didn't record it immediately. Trying for a baby isn't always sunshine and roses—especially after two years of hopeful attempts.

"I'm going to pick up Wendy," Kai said.

"Wait!" I rolled off the bed and rummaged around for my under-wear in the sheets.

"You stay, wait for Mr. G to get home." He disappeared into the kitchen.

"But—" I followed him, naked and all. The cold tile floor sent chills from my bare feet up to my legs.

"I know how long you've been waiting to find Carlo." My husband yanked on a pair of shoes. He offered me a smile that turned into a smirk as his gaze dropped to my bare boobs. Thank goodness he couldn't see the hood and neither of us could feel it—unless I willed it. That'd certainly mess with sexy time.

"It's probably good I don't go, anyway. The security guard will just kick me out again."

"Wait, what?" Kai paused in the doorway. The footsteps that echoed from the hall had me leaping behind the counter to hide my naked body from a passerby.

"Tell you later!" I called from behind the counter. Only my eyes peeked above the edge of the counter like a frog in a pond. That was one fairy tale I had yet to encounter, though I wished I would. I'd kiss a frog if it meant I could get pregnant again. *I don't think that's how that works.* But the hood felt like a curse and maybe that meant wishes came true too.

"Love you," Kai shouted before the door slammed shut.

If only our love was enough to bring forth a child. I stood alone in the empty apartment and placed my palm on my flat stomach.

My throat squeezed.

From the bedroom, my phone dinged. I took a shuddering breath and shook my head before retrieving the phone.

Kai: That was Mr. G and Tala in the hall. Also, we need groceries, so I'll take Wendy shopping with me. Be home around dinner.

I threw on one of Kai's T-shirts that read *I'm a cool dad* and a pair of jeans. On the way across the hall, I shot Scarlet a text about the Pinocchio sighting on TV. Her lack of response must have meant my boss was working her extra hard this week. Scarlet had officially started interning at Bay Side Media a year and a half ago. She earned a small wage that kept her afloat while the opportunity taught her about investigative journalism.

My knuckles knocked against Mr. Geppetto's front door, and Tala's warm smile greeted me from the other side. Thankfully, the only glow coming from her was the bright face of a caffeinated woman in love. Since they'd started dating, she moved with a skip in her step despite joint problems and heavy legs.

"Come in," she said, moving out of the door frame. "Joseph and I just returned from a visit to that new cafe on Main. They have a delightful dinner menu."

Mr. Geppetto emerged from the kitchen in the back of the one-bedroom condo with a glass of water. "We had to convince them to let us order off the dinner menu during lunch hour."

Ah, yes, I needed to remember the older couple's bedtime was earlier than Wendy's.

"Well, don't let me interrupt your date," I said. "This will be quick."

Tala gestured for me to sit down in an overstuffed chair across from the two rockers where the elderly couple perched. Since his daughter's death, Mr. Geppetto seemed to age rapidly, giving in to the retired luxury of excessive sleep.

"I'm investigating a murder," I lied. These two didn't need to know about the thin veil between the fictional world full of monsters and our own—also full of monsters. I pulled out my phone and tapped on the screenshot I'd saved from the video streaming across news networks. "I'm hoping you might recognize this young man. Maybe he hung out with Katarina." The mention of his daughter's name caused him to wince. I didn't enjoy hurting him, but finding Pinocchio and ultimately Johnson could save a lot of lives if it helped me understand the story cycle better. No more successful escapes by Evil Queens or watching Ugly Ducklings suffer until they ultimately commit suicide. The old investigations sent a shudder through me.

Mr. Geppetto leaned forward in his rocking chair and pulled his glasses down from the top of his head. Hair poked out of his nostrils as he scrunched his nose and squinted at the small screen. A slight pinch appeared between his salt and pepper eyebrows and I could have sworn recognition flickered as his pupils expanded.

He shook his head and relaxed against the back of the wooden chair again. "I apologize, Mari, I can't help you."

I tilted my head. Mr. Geppetto wouldn't meet my gaze. Did he forget I interviewed serial killers for my job? I knew the tells.

Can't help me? Or won't? And why not? This was all so weird, and that said a lot coming from the chick who watched her mother transform into a swan.

"This is important, please. A car hit him and he's missing now. It could help find a killer." It wasn't a total lie. Johnson could have killed a person or two.

Mr. Geppetto gazed out the window beside his chair. Pedestrians milled about on the street below. As his jaw shifted back and forth, I guessed at the battle between truth and lies within him.

"His name is Carlo," I said, hoping to jog a buried memory. "I thought I'd heard you say that name before." Not a lie, though I didn't know when or why he'd said it. Maybe it was my imagination.

His lips twitched, then he took a long inhale, eyes never leaving the outside scene.

"Joseph?" Tala laid her hand on his arm.

The light streaming in from the window cast an angelic glow around him. I blinked to double-check that it wasn't the story aura descending on an innocent old man.

Mr. Geppetto yanked away from his girlfriend's touch. She squeaked in shock. The reaction softened his tense jaw muscles, and he reached for her hand.

"I'm sorry, my love," he said. "I forgot what we were talking about."

I narrowed my eyes. He'd glanced to the left when he said it and used his free hand to palm at gathering beads of sweat along his receded hairline. All signs of someone not telling the truth.

What the hell?

Tala took her other hand and squeezed his with both of hers. "He worries me so."

When Mr. Geppetto lifted her hands, he brought them to his lips, and he kissed her like she was a queen. His unfriendly frown and glance at me told me I was the nosy kingdom intruding on their privacy.

"Well," I said, standing. "If either of you remembers seeing Carlo anywhere, you know I'm just across the hall."

Tala showed me out and I dragged myself back to our door, defeated. It had been two years of no clues, no answers, and no positive pregnancy tests.

I pushed through the door and flopped on the couch. Staring up at the ceiling reminded me of the struggles of breastfeeding and the moment I first saw an article about the wolf's attack. That was long before I knew about supernatural creatures and the fictional world coming to life. I was so innocent then, a brand-new, clueless (no pun intended) mom. Not only had I not been ready for motherhood, but I also wasn't ready for the truth that I'd become Red Riding Hood, and my rude coworker had turned into a wolf thirsty for my blood.

I'd survived then, I would survive now. No way would I let the hood control me. I straightened, scooted to the edge of the couch, and grabbed a block of Post-It notes. By the time Kai arrived home with Wendy, the Coffee Table of Evidence had returned to its full glory. Colorful notes stuck to the tabletop with scribbled clues and ideas. If I called the search for Carlo and Johnson a murder investigation, I would treat it like one.

Dishes clattered, and cabinets banged in the kitchen after Kai agreed to whip up breakfast for dinner. I'd already tried ordering Door-Dash too many times. Carlo never delivered, and we were about to go broke over mobile food orders. A plate of hot pancakes covered the notes in front of me.

"Pause and eat with us," Kai said, as he plopped into the side chair.

Wendy shoveled cheese-saturated scrambled eggs into her mouth. She sat on her knees and ate at the coffee table with us. I had no problem dropping the investigation for my daughter.

"Tell me all about your first day of preschool."

Wendy shrugged. "My friend says the police took you."

My heart skipped a beat at the memory of jail. I'd been torn from my baby and tossed in a cell under suspicion of cold-blooded murder.

"But I told him my mommy is a police."

Not entirely untrue from her perspective. I worked with Detective Wilhelm often and researched cases like an officer.

Bacon crunched as Wendy took a bite. "'Cept you're not a police like my school police. He just stands around out front."

I breathed, relieved at the realization that she wasn't referring to my actual arrest—just the incident with the security guard earlier.

"My friend has two baby sisters," she said in between sips of apple juice. I leaned across the table and brushed Wendy's unruly auburn hair from her freckled face. The syrup from her pancakes had already stuck to the wispy ends. "I want a baby brother."

I'd take the skipped beat back over a cracked heart. My palm flew to my chest, and I frowned, exchanging sad glances with Kai.

"We'd like that too, Wednesday." He called her by her nickname. "But there are some things we just can't control."

Not if I have anything to do with it. I planned to control it so hard, doubling down on tracking my cycle and organizing both those notes and the ones pertaining to the investigation.

"My friend says he got two presents when his sisters first got born." Wendy dug into her stack of fluffy pancakes.

Kai laughed and said something about how she just wanted the presents, not the sibling. It was likely intended to ease my pain on the subject, but I didn't pay attention. My brain already dove into intense organization mode. For the future of our family, I'd make it to our appointment with a fertility specialist and follow all of their tips to perfection.

And for the future of the story cycle, I'd throw myself into the deep end and live inside books until I understood the fictional world better. Maybe then I'd be able to track down Carlo and Johnson. I'd accept nothing less.

After I shoved the pancakes away, I stood and stepped over Kai's legs. Flour and sugar weren't healthy enough to promote a fertile environment inside my body.

"Won't you eat?" he asked.

I shook my head, and he stabbed my rejected pancakes with his fork.

"It'll interfere with my immersion."

"What does that mean?" My husband looked up at me with an expression twisted in confusion.

I marched around the coffee table and crouched at the cube-shaped shelves beneath the TV stand. Stacks of books filled my arms that I'd used to cross reference with online sources about the origins and first-edition versions of fairy tales.

"Haven't you ever heard of method acting?" I asked. I turned and balanced the stack between my hands and my chin. "I'm going to live in these stories until I stop the cycle for good."

Kai swallowed, his throat bobbing. A crease of concern dented the space between his brow. "Isn't that a little ambitious?"

"It's not ambitious enough. Besides, I'm useless right now. Our daughter is growing up, and she doesn't need me like she used to. I'm off work, plus Scarlet has taken over a lot of my responsibilities, and I'm doing more harm than good with the hood right now." I dumped the books I planned to immerse myself in on the couch. I flipped open the closest one with Jack and his oversized beanstalk. After a refresher on that, I moved to Lewis Carrol's *Alice's Adventures in Wonderland*. The colorful illustrations immediately pulled me in. I skimmed the surface of the story, reminding myself of Alice's dangerous journey through the arbitrary and abstract world of Wonderland until Kai called for me to get our daughter ready for her adventures in sleepland.

After a goodnight routine with Wendy, I stood in the doorway and leaned against the frame. Wendy went to bed early, zoning out quickly after her first day at school. I hummed "Mary Had Little Lamb" and fought back tears—determination didn't make the emotions go away.

I sighed. The real world had little to offer me right now. When Kai came up behind me and snaked his arms around my waist, I welcomed the suggestion of his warm kiss on the back of my neck. Roleplay first, then immersion. Both would distract me from the crappy truths of my current life status.

For the second time that day, Kai threw on a chest-revealing blouse. We tumbled and gasped and accused each other of stealing treasure as if we were pirates having enemies-to-lovers sex on a stolen boat.

My husband propped his head in his hand and eyed me as I stood to pull on pajamas. "What happened to immersion? We took an hour chunk out of your story study time."

I circled my palm around my stomach, bunching the t-shirt I'd just pulled on. "Stories and sex. That will be my life from now on. I'm going to end the cycle and start a baby."

Kai stood and flicked the light on in the attached bathroom. "You make our future baby sound like a lawnmower."

"You're right, ending the cycle is too far-fetched right now. I need to deconstruct how it works first." I tapped my chin. After snatching a blanket from the foot of our bed, I turned to head out of the room.

"Are we having two different conversations?" Kai spoke to my back's reflection in the bathroom mirror.

By the time he took a shower, threw on some sweatpants, and found his phone, I'd redecorated our living room. Kai froze at the edge of the kitchen tile and double-backed, as if he were about to fall over a cliff.

Sticky notes covered the living room floor like colorful landmines, each unique with its own scribbled piece of information. The Coffee Table of Evidence had exploded, leaving casualties from the entry to the kitchen.

"Did I time travel?" Kai asked as he pointed behind him at the bedroom. "I could have sworn I was only in the shower for ten minutes."

I crawled across the carpet on my hands and knees the way Wendy used to. It was another obnoxious reminder that she wasn't my baby anymore.

"I've been collecting these notes," I said. "The red Post-Its contain all the information Scarlet knows about the cycle. The orange is my research and the yellow are your historical facts that line up with the stories."

Kai tiptoed into the room, dodging the pieces of paper to make it to

Couch Island. He flopped on the cushions and pointed to the small section of blue notes. "What are these?"

"Everything we know about Johnson." I sighed. "And the few green ones are about Carlo, or Pinocchio, or whatever we should call him. What sucks is that I can gather all this information, but it doesn't fix that I'm not helping anyone as the Keeper. But I'm not saying Scarlet was any better. She did this for hundreds of years, and a lot of people died."

Wet hair fell into Kai's face, and he shook it away like a dog. When it didn't work, he raked his fingers through his hair and slick it back over his head. "But you can twist the violent stories."

"So the person who was unlucky enough to become the villain just gets the boot?" I shook my head. "I'm not a murderer, Kai."

He exaggerated relief by wiping imaginary sweat from his forehead.

"Even if the story aura lands on someone with aggressive tendencies, who am I to decide they should die first? What if people can fight the aura somehow? What if Johnson has even a fraction more information than we do?" I scooted toward the coffee table to scribble another note about Johnson. *Real body teleported into a virtual world.*

"You have your obsessive eyes on," Kai said. "We'll keep trying to find him, but you can only control what you can control."

"Insightful." I shot him an unimpressed look. "I don't get like that anymore. Plus, I'm not organizing everything to control it, I'm doing it to immerse myself. I've always had one foot out the door with the Keeper's responsibilities, and now it's time to dive into the deep end. I'm going to do this my way and—"

A knock rapped at the door.

We exchanged looks with each other before Kai rose and darted from Couch Island to the escape route.

"Tell Scar she has to wipe her shoes before she comes inside," I said.

"Wendy doesn't crawl anymore, we don't need to worry—" Kai cut himself off before saying something silly. It was a reflex to remind

Scar to keep our house free of small objects and dirt from Wendy's babyhood.

Now the Post-Its are my babies. Kidding.

But at least it distracted me from the baby I didn't have. One child was growing up, while the other was nonexistent and out of reach. Pain lanced through my chest.

"I have a confession." A deep voice that definitely didn't belong to Scarlet said from the open door.

I looked up to see our neighbor uncomfortably rubbing the back of his hand with his other thumb and his thick brows pinched. Age spots dotted the skin of his hands and forehead. Mr. Geppetto stepped inside the entry as Kai moved aside.

"We need a boat to get to the couch," Kai joked.

Mr. Geppetto didn't laugh. "That boy from the news…" his voice trailed as he glanced at our sliding glass door that overlooked the street. "Is he in some kind of trouble? Or is he hurt?"

"Carlo?" I stood now, recognizing guilt on the old man's face. "He's missing."

"Do you know him?" Kai asked. He tilted his head, but Mr. Geppetto didn't meet his gaze.

Instead, our neighbor sighed and scrubbed his forehead with his open palm. "I lied earlier when I told you I didn't recognize him."

My heart flip-flopped. Another piece of the puzzle was finally within my grasp after two years of searching.

"Where do you know him from?" I peeled off a blank sticky note from the block of green and pressed the pen to paper until the ink bled.

"That's what's tricky," he said, glancing between us. Mr. Geppetto shook his head. When he frowned, the loose skin of his chin hung like a hound dog. "Tala is worried I'm showing signs of dementia and I'm beginning to believe her."

Kai frowned and shot me a look that said, *you've got your obsessive eyes on.* I couldn't let Mr. Geppetto become a casualty in my quest for knowledge, so I said nothing. This man had suffered enough after his daughter died to the wolf—more proof the story cycle needed to be shut down for good. Even when Scarlet was the Keeper of Stories, she made mistakes and loads of poor choices.

I didn't intend for the silence to prod him into speaking again. I'd used the tactic in interviews, but it wasn't one I'd ever put on my friendly old neighbor.

"The boy is from a game," he said, the strange confession spilling from his lips. But it wasn't strange to us at all.

Kai visibly perked up, and it encouraged Mr. Geppetto.

"I know it's odd for a man my age, but I've taken to playing video games when my eyes can handle it. Sometimes it gives me a headache, but I enjoy keeping my mind sharp with all the learning involved."

"Why don't you come in and sit down," I said, waving for him to take a seat on the chair angled beside the couch. "Just step on the notes."

Kai gasped, and I rolled my eyes at his dramatics.

Mr. Geppetto continued as he made his way to the chair. "Tala would think I've lost my marbles if she heard me say this." A groan escaped him as he took a seat and the cushion sank beneath his weight. "I knew the missing boy from Fortress Clash."

"The game!" Kai snapped his fingers and pointed.

"Is that what that is?" I glanced between them. The name of the game had changed since I'd written the article about Carlo. Mr. Geppetto furrowed the bushes hanging over his eyes.

"Yep." My husband smirked. "A video game."

Oh yeah, it's all coming together. My jaw dropped before I grinned. Our poor neighbor likely thought us insane for the excitement at his answer.

"Are you mocking me?" Mr. Geppetto asked. It took some strain that showed by the protruding vein on his temple, but he stood again and shook his head.

"No!" I said, as I danced across the sticky notes and landed my hand on his forearm. He turned to meet my gaze, eyes darkened with frustration. "We're not. I swear."

His mustache bristled as he curled his lip. "It's not dementia."

"We believe you," Kai said.

"We need to find Carlo," I added. The muscle in his arm finally relaxed, and Mr. Geppetto sank back into the chair. I backed up and perched on the edge of the couch, never taking my eyes off the old man as if he could disappear and take my answers with him. It wasn't a crazy thought because Johnson had disappeared. Hell, Scarlet, when she was the woman in the red cloak, vanished into portals too many times to count. I was tired of dealing with impossible investigations when the suspects and clues skipped away into unreachable places.

My reflex was to reach out and snatch Mr. Geppetto's hand before a rabbit hole opened in the center of our living room and squirreled him away. When I found his warm hand, it comforted me more than I expected. Something about this other world, this Fortress Clash, gave me a sense of excitement I couldn't explain. I refused to let him go there without me.

"I wish I could be of more help," he said.

"Can you tell us how to find Carlo?"

Mr. Geppetto's throat bobbed, then his lips twisted into a frown that pulled at his leathery tan skin. "I think you misunderstood." He sighed and licked his lips. "Carlo isn't a player of the game. He's a character *in* the game."

It sounded a little nutty. Which was right up my alley—especially if you asked Miss Jenna. I dealt in crazy lately. I took a bath in it, and I wanted to stay in that bath because crazy was better than reality right now.

Kai nodded. *Are you thinking what I'm thinking?* My brain connected the dots in an array of colors. Fortress Clash plus Carlo equaled locating Johnson. And once we found Johnson and pried answers from him, maybe the story cycle would change. Maybe I'd stop failing.

Maybe I'd give him the hood.

I shook my head, jarring the insane thought to the back of my mind from where it would nag me. *How dare you even think it!*

I took a deep breath.

"Do you still play Fortress Clash?" I asked.

Mr. Geppetto grumbled something about a waste of time, but a flicker of light in his eye betrayed him. Tala may have rescued him from a sedentary life of gaming, but he may not have considered it a rescue.

"My computer needs updates, but I remember my password if that's what you—"

"Use ours," Kai said. He dipped across the living room, finally gaining the courage to step on my sticky notes. His quick glance at me told me he didn't make the decision lightly. I only shook my head.

The large work laptop covered half the coffee table. Kai cracked it open and pulled up the login for Fortress Clash on the webpage.

"I know this sounds crazy," I said, "but locating him in the game could help us find him." *And I'm dying to try something new.* The bartender's comment about living in a simulation came back to me. *This* world felt like a simulation, a universe of uncontrollable monsters, and predictable stories that broke the rules. Here, Mr. Darcy and Elizabeth were on the brink of divorce. Quasimodo was going to die no matter what I did. Evil Queens got away with murder, and the princes drowned their sorrows in frozen Walmart TV dinners.

Take me somewhere else.

"Well then, I'd be glad to help," Mr. Geppetto said, as he straightened. "But I'll need my VR equipment."

VR? I mouthed.

"Virtual reality." Kai pantomimed putting a headset over his face.

When he returned, Mr. Geppetto carried a heavy, white piece of equipment. The headset looked like something straight out of a science fiction movie. Good ol' Geordi La Forge would be proud. Where is Scarlet to quote Star Trek when you need her?

"All right," he said, "let's see if we can find him."

A dissonant, eerie tune rolled from the laptop's speakers as the game booted up. Mr. Geppetto eased the headset on and clicked a controller in his hand.

A woman's voice echoed from the speakers. I arched an eyebrow at Kai as he flinched at the volume. He turned it down, but not before the character greeted the player.

"You must be mad to join the fight," she said.

Mr. Geppetto clicked a button that I could only assume signed him into the world.

He chuckled to himself. "Yes, I'm over eighteen years old."

"Must be a spooky game," Kai said.

"Violent at times," Mr. Geppetto answered. "Carlo is a non-player character, which means they built him into the game. He's not a character that you or I can use to navigate the game. His location changes so this could take some time."

I willed my leg to stop bouncing. While I waited, I grabbed my phone and shot a text to Scar.

Hey, we might have found the world Carlo lives in. But that doesn't explain the car accident and the vanishing body. Have you found anything?

The music from the loading screen faded and the woman's too-calm voice returned.

"Now that you have joined, you are among us. We're all mad here. Welcome to Fortress Clash."

Chapter 4

In Hot Water

We were in trouble. Like grounded for a year, no phone or TV trouble. Or we would be if Tala were our mother and us, her teenagers. It almost felt that way when she'd found us huddled around Mr. Geppetto and his trek into Fortress Clash.

Tala had wagged a scolding finger at all three of us, and more or less demanded that we stop with the bad influence on her boyfriend. Unfortunately for her, we didn't listen. Mr. Geppetto silently agreed to return the next day when his overprotective girlfriend had a knitting club at her friend's house.

Everything about the plan felt silly. Three adults sneaking around to play a video game didn't match my usual workday business. But I'd taken a vacation, and this wasn't work—it was a matter of life or death. My life anyway.

I couldn't die with the hood. Could I also not create life while wearing it?

I forced the smoothie Kai had made down my throat and pulled myself to sit on the kitchen counter.

After another text to Scarlet, I scrolled through Fortress Clash forums. Angry players argued with one another about the answers to a quest in the game. Another group claimed they'd wandered into a forbidden part of the game's map that was never meant to be seen by players. Apparently, it had a deck of cards that moved and walked around as non-player characters. When they entered the area, one player was selected at random to have his head cut off.

I cringed and clicked on a different thread. This section spoke of the forbidden area, too. The beheading didn't occur this time. Instead, the players reported being blocked from the area. An invisible barrier stopped their characters from moving into a clearing in the field. They could see it and even capture in-game snapshots of the area, but couldn't go there. The pictures showed bright colors clashed with the usual browns and muted greens of the medieval-style game. In a distant field, a long table covered in decadent food was buried by tall grass. The forums insisted it was impossible to reach the table.

I had no clue what any of this meant or how it would relate to Pinocchio and Johnson, but if there was a forbidden area, perhaps he was hiding there.

Kai burst through the door, heavy bags in hand. More bags hung from his wrists and forearms as he lumbered his way into the living room. Mr. Geppetto followed behind. The two men set to work, setting up the VR equipment and logging into the game.

"I got more so we can watch!" Kai showed me two boxes of brand new headsets.

A rush of adrenaline sent me hopping off the counter and snatching the box from his hand. Even the promise of escape into the wild world of Fortress Clash couldn't get my mind off Wendy, but it'd help a little.

"How'd she do today?" I asked as I pulled the headset out of the carboard. "Did she miss me? Did the teacher say anything?"

Kai shrugged. "She said you're one peanut short of a trail mix. And by she, I mean our daughter."

"What?"

"Mari, I'm kidding."

I swatted his arm, but he dodged away, so I tossed the empty headset box at his feet. Kai danced on one foot and pretended to be injured from the attack.

"Ready kids?" Mr. Geppetto interrupted our battle.

He logged into his account while we selected to spectate his in-game name. The headset added about twenty pounds to my head. Note to self: never get on the scale while in a virtual reality world.

"This is just the lobby," he said.

His character moved on the screen and it felt like this version of him was right in front of me. I could reach out and touch him. Of course, I'd feel nothing. A glittering beige mist floated around Mr. Geppetto's character and gave him a magical glow. Did that come from the game, or had he designed his character to look that way? I didn't know a lot about video games or virtual reality, but I knew players could tweak the look of their character however they wanted. Mr. Geppetto appeared to be partial to magical-looking properties.

The character's movements were fluid and quick. He opened a door and exited the lobby area. The outside was dim, a night street in an old town. A castle stood in the distance. Another player ran by with a funny name hovering over their head and a sword at their hip.

We'd stepped into a medieval world.

"This isn't a safe place anymore," Mr. Geppetto said. He moved into the space, passing bodies on the cobblestone street. The dark mounds disappeared from our line of sight as he followed a path that led toward the castle. "Everything has changed."

"What does that mean?" I asked.

"It looks like they're wiping out the original servers and bringing in different content."

It was just as Carlo had predicted. But when we'd met him, Carlo claimed to have created the world. So why was he just a non-player character in the game?

"We're inside the main fortress right now," Mr. Geppetto explained. "Guilds gather here. It's supposed to be a safe space where no fighting occurs, but those bodies prove otherwise. I'll head to the castle. The queen's character always knows where the court jester is."

"Is that Carlo?"

Mr. Geppetto used his character to send me a thumbs up. "The court jester always has insider information that you'd typically use to trade to solve quests and level up."

Once he made it to the castle, he sighed again. "This is all different. I don't know where to go from here. I can't even move to the court's east wing, almost like it doesn't even exist. The game is being erased, and I don't know if I'll be able to find the jester."

Mr. Geppetto's character stopped halfway down a hallway in the castle. Though it appeared non-player characters milled past the stopping point, he couldn't move toward them.

"This is very odd. Usually, the jester would be in the throne room, but we can't even get to the doorway."

"Just go there," I prodded.

"The game won't let me."

A mist floated in the air in front of his character. It disappeared into the room he'd pointed out as the throne room. The dirt color of it should have matched the rest of the dim world, but it clashed, as if separate from the game.

"You have to go in there," I said.

The character bumped into an invisible barrier as Mr. Geppetto clicked a button to walk forward. "We'll speak with the king when night falls, and he moves to his chambers. Maybe the jester will be with him then."

"Don't you see that? It's a trail leading you into that room." My voice cracked, hysterical with frustration. *Just click the stupid buttons and move your character!*

"There's no trail," Kai said. "I don't know what you added to your smoothie this morning, but I'm feeling left out."

"Just let me do it." I pulled off my headset. "I mean, will you let me try?"

Mr. Geppetto and Kai followed suit. "You want to play on my account?"

"I just want to show you what I'm seeing." I slipped the headset back on. On the stone wall beside Mr. Geppetto's character, a scroll appeared. It was tucked in between the stones and pressed deep into the wall. Only the end of it was visible because of the frayed edges. It would have meant nothing to me if the glittering brown mist didn't circle it. Was this what the story aura looked like in-game? "There's something new! Can you pull that out?"

Mr. Geppetto returned to the game and plucked the scroll from the wall. He unrolled it to reveal a scribbled message.

I'm stuck in the game. The server is being erased and I can't find my body. I'm going to die. Help me find my way out! -C

"It's him," I said, sure of the story's glow and what the message didn't say. *I was a real boy once, and now I'm trapped in the game.* Of course, Pinocchio would surface as a creepy virtual reality character, because why would my job as the Keeper of Stories be easy? That'd be nuts. Nothing was easy. "We have to find him. He's trapped and it'll kill him."

Finally, I'll do something good with the hood.

"It's just a game," Mr. Geppetto said.

"No, he's inside the game," I argued. "His consciousness or something, I don't know. Just let me play."

I ripped off the headset, but it snagged on my earring and pulled too hard. I yelped. Mr. Geppetto and Kai exchanged glances that told me more than I cared to know.

"Let me play." I reached for Mr. Geppetto's headset. "Please, will you allow me to try?" I cringed, more so at his likely refusal than my awkward, desperate behavior.

Kai leaned toward our neighbor, never taking his eyes off of me. "One peanut short of a trail mix."

My shoulders slumped, and I shot him the look of death. Before he could mouth, 'I'm kidding,' Mr. Geppetto shrugged and handed me his headset.

"You're welcome to try, but please stay within the fortress. It took me hundreds of hours to level this account."

I grabbed the headset and pulled it over my head. He placed the controllers into my hands and I moved the character's body with my own.

"This is weird."

The mist was clearer from the character's point of view. It trailed back down the hall and out of the castle. Mr. Geppetto instructed me on how to speed up the character's walk as I followed the story aura.

Maybe I'd take back what I said about it being easy. Never had the aura been so unmistakable before. It'd take me right to the missing boy, then we'd find out what happened to his body from where he logged in, I'd give Pinocchio his realness back, and I'd be a hero. Hera? No, that was a Greek goddess—one I needed to channel to get my dusty old womb in gear.

I jogged from the castle, past other players, street merchants, and handcarts. A large gate signaled the end of the massive wall that surrounded the beginning area.

"Wait, you're leaving the safe zone!" Mr. Geppetto said.

The mist grew thicker and brighter, as if the in-game sun reflected off the story aura. I followed it into a field.

"It's just a meadow," I said, defeated. I shuffled through the tall grass, hoping to stumble over a character's body, but the story aura trail had gone cold. The character shivered and goosebumps prickled on my arm as if I could feel the chill of the evening air from the game.

"You need to get back into the fortress before nightfall."

"Just give me a little longer," I said, not ready to give up the search. "What about this forest?" I dragged the character between the trees. Patches of weak moonlight shone through the heavy overhang of leaves.

"You'll die from an animal or exposure," Mr. Geppetto said.

"Okay, I'll go back, but I don't know which way I came in."

The bits of light didn't help. I could barely see the character's hand in front of me. The crunch of leaves muffled the faint sound of metal on metal.

"What was that?" Kai asked. "You need to get out of there, Mari. You're going to lose all of his character's stuff."

"Uh." The words hung in my throat. I may have acted impulsively and didn't have a clue how to find my way back. But if I gave the control back to Mr. Geppetto, he'd return the character to safety. And who cares about a stupid game character when a boy's life was on the line? I was the Keeper, I could save him.

Plus, who said I wanted to go back? I was getting the hang of the controllers, and a few lost items were worth a continued search. The items weren't real, anyway. None of it was—except for Carlo.

I swung my arms and tried to move the character but it wouldn't budge.

"It's frozen."

The metal on metal echoed again until a sickening gurgling sound followed. Pain lanced up between my ribcage from my stomach while air sucked from my lungs. I stumbled backward, my balance off because of the heavy headset.

"What was that? What happened?" Kai asked.

The character's body collapsed on the forest floor, his face partially visible in a patch of light. Dark red blood spilled from his mouth.

I ripped the headset off and fell into the chair beside the couch. My throat and chest squeezed so tight I couldn't gasp even a pinch of air.

The sharp pain throbbed into a dull ache just below my sternum.

"Mari?" Kai threw off his headset and scrambled to kneel beside my chair. "What's wrong?"

I opened my mouth, but no words came out.

If Johnson could go into the virtual world, maybe I could too. Maybe I did, partially. I swallowed and sucked in just enough breath to whisper what had happened.

"The game tried to kill me."

Chapter 5

The Tip of the Iceberg

Killing the Keeper? Not possible. Immortality existed because of the hood. And my life a hopeless eternity of hunting fairy tale monsters.

"I'm so sorry," I told Mr. Geppetto for the hundredth time. He shook his head and held out his palm. He might have had a tear in his eye, but I couldn't see since he turned away and marched for the door. "How can I make it up to you?"

Mr. Geppetto paused in the doorway, the same place Scarlet stood several years ago. The place I'd tried to trap her with an anti-portal spell. Where was she today?

"Find the boy," he said. "That's how you can make it up to me. Fortress Clash forces accounts with dead characters to wait for a grieving period before making another character. Please, just leave my account alone."

"Yes, sir." I saluted, but our neighbor only shook his head at me.

Kai closed the door behind him and spun around. "Are you sure your chest doesn't hurt anymore? What if it was a mini heart attack? We're getting older, you know."

I didn't answer. I was already pulling the headset over my face again. Plus, I didn't need to sit around and think about how I'd aged.

My body reminded me of that often enough with its lack of a baby in the womb. But I'd kept up with my health and the last my doctor said, I was as fertile as a Felicia on prom night.

It had to be the fault of the hood.

"Mari!" Kai's voice squeaked. "Mr. G just asked you to leave his account alone. Use the other headset or log out."

"I don't know how." I shook my head. "I won't hurt anything."

"You have got to be kidding me. You just killed his level billion character and you're going to do exactly what he asked you not to. What the hell has gotten into you?"

I yanked the headset off and dropped it in the chair behind me. "It doesn't matter. The account is on hold, like he said."

Kai picked it up and peered at the screen without pulling the whole device over his head. Instead of the forest or the character's body, the screen was black with a plain coffin spinning in the center. Below a loading symbol of two clashing swords, it read *Grieving Period over in 47:22 hours.*

I dropped onto the couch and dragged the other headset off the coffee table.

"What're you doing?" Kai asked. "I thought now that we have some alone time…"

I let the headset fall from my hands to the cushion on the couch and folded my arms. "You're thinking about sex at a time like this?"

"I'm thinking about your ovulation window…"

I steepled my fingers and pursed my lips. He wasn't wrong. The window opened for a specific amount of time and our doctor had encouraged us to track it carefully. It was supposed to help us conceive, though, that had proven useless so far. Each time my period came half a day late, I rushed out to purchase a pregnancy test. And each time, the pregnancy test displayed only one sad, lone little line.

I shook my head, not wanting to think about another failure of mine. I couldn't get pregnant, couldn't save those whose free will was stripped by the fairy tale aura and couldn't get over the fact that my daughter was growing up.

Not to mention I'd lost my mother and would soon lose my best friend to the stories. Mom flew away, never to return, and Esmeralda was slowly falling for Reese—AKA Quasimodo—no matter how hard I tried to dissuade her.

The cushion sunk in beside me. Kai took a seat and bumped my shoulder with his.

"What happened to my organized Pulitzer-prize-seeking wife?"

I pinched my brow and glared at him. Apparently, the expression looked threatening because he threw up his hands in mock surrender, but his words didn't follow.

"The Mari I know doesn't ping-pong from obsessively covering the floor in notes to diving into a video game. You're all over the place."

I scrubbed my palms over my face, then swiped the hair away. Wispy, escaped strands fell back into my eyes, tickling my cheeks. I grunted and adjusted the half-ponytail with another twist tighter from the hair tie.

"This is the opposite of how you typically set your mind to something until you solve it," Kai said.

"Don't you get it?" I picked up the headset again and twirled the wire around my finger. "I *can't* solve this. No matter how much good I try to do with the hood, it comes back around to bite me in the butt. But with this, I can help Carlo, and I don't have to push him to marry someone he doesn't like or tear him away from the love of his life."

"Forget Mr. Darcy and Elizabeth for a minute—"

"What about Reese and Esme?" I tilted my head at him. "Their choices are to fall in love and die or be torn apart and live forever with a hole in their hearts."

Kai's shoulders slumped. He wasn't winning this one, but it didn't stop him from trying to dig out the positive buried under mounds of red fabric. "You freed your mom—"

"And now she's gone forever." I interrupted.

"You saved your own life and brought down a serial killer." Kai shifted to face me, determined now that he'd won.

"Ah, yes, something that I could have done as a trained professional who tracks and interviews serial killers to keep the city safe. The hood isn't a blessing."

He snapped his fingers and shook his head. The battle had only just begun, and I'd come with an arsenal. Too many sleepless nights left me wondering about what life would be like without the hood. Who out there could be a better Keeper of Stories?

"Frankenstein—"

"Killed himself, I did nothing," I interrupted.

Kai curled his hands into fists and drummed them on the coffee table. The motion was likely to jog up a few ideas—which meant he was running out.

"You stopped Heath from creating new stories that would have gotten people killed."

I let my head fall back as I looked up at the ceiling. "Okay…" I didn't have a comeback for that one yet.

"A-hah!" Kai pumped his fist into the air. "Victory is mine."

I launched forward, straightening in the seat. With one finger in the air, I shushed his celebratory jiggle. "In the process of stopping Heath, I took off the hood, which means hundreds of thousands of stories from this century will start tearing through the fabric of reality into the next century."

"And by then you'll be queen of the world, Mari the fairy tale monster terminator—" he beamed.

"By then I'll be broken because everyone I love will be dead."

Kai's smile vanished, but his look wasn't one of sadness. I didn't defeat his positivity, only inspired disappointment.

"Fine." He shrugged. "Be negative. But the go-getter woman I know doesn't find every excuse she can to ignore reality."

"Is that why you think I want to go into the video game?" My jaw dropped as my body stood. I folded my arms and stared down at him.

"Isn't it?" He met my gaze. "First it was pretending you'd help in Wendy's classroom, then you only wanted roleplay sex. Then it was all about diving into books and stories to study. Now the game. But reality is right here, Mari!"

"Oh, really?" I shook my head. "You think I can't see what's right in front of me?"

He stood, placing himself in the very space we discussed—right in front of my face. Kai's unique scent pricked my heart. Now wasn't the time, but his lips looked so inviting. The fire burning in my chest told me I'd melt him in one touch.

"You can see it just fine," he said. "You just don't want to accept it."

Rage flickered and, if I didn't know better, I'd say pregnancy heartburn was back.

"Why are you trying to convince me not to go after Pinocchio?" I asked.

His face twisted in confusion. "I'm not. I'm just worried about you—"

"Well, don't!" I did enough worrying for both of us. Wendy needed one grounded parent, and I couldn't give that to her.

"You can't control me, Mari." Kai stepped into the space between us, putting his face inches from mine.

"I don't want to."

"That's a lie," he said, his breath on my neck.

I couldn't take it anymore. Maybe I did want to control him. Without thinking, I grabbed his face in my hands and kissed him until I couldn't breathe. My fingers found the back of his neck and climbed up to twist into his hair. He lifted me and my legs instinctively wrapped around his waist.

Kai carried me toward the bedroom, where I pushed him away from me. He stumbled back and sat on the edge of the mattress while I paced.

"You tricked me so I wouldn't go back to the game, didn't you?"

His lips curved into a smirk. Kai bit his lip, but it didn't stop the laugh that followed.

"Was the fight even real?" I asked.

"Mari, you've done a lot of good with the hood."

"Right, well, time to do more and save Pinocchio." I plopped down beside him.

"Okay, but this is unfamiliar territory. You don't understand virtual reality."

"Excuse me—"

"So I'm going with you," he demanded in a voice that definitely got me hot and bothered all over again.

The determination in his voice stopped me short. It wouldn't be the first time Kai put himself on a mission with me. We'd lured out the wolf together. He'd taken the brunt of the wolf's attack while I'd stolen the hood from Scarlet.

"What are you worried about, Kai? I can't die."

"Your body can't in our world," he said, "but this is new and the fact that you felt it when the character got stabbed is proof you're at risk. Not to mention Carlo is inside the game. We met the guy, the real, flesh and blood dude before, and now his consciousness is, what, a non-player character in a disappearing game? What if that happens to you?"

Immortality did weird things to a girl. There I was, never considering death. The concept had vanished from my peripheral. But my poor husband hadn't forgotten and the look on his face told me he was picturing a life of raising Wendy without me.

I brushed my thumb along his jawline and dropped my head into the space between his shoulder and neck.

"Okay, you're right," I said. "Your parents are picking Wendy up from preschool tomorrow. So, we can both go into the game then."

Kai nodded. "This'll be a weird anniversary trip."

I laughed and sunk into the warmth of my husband's body. We had a day left in my ovulation window. Might as well take advantage of it.

Chapter 6

Clear as Mud

I sighed and set the phone on the table. The detective was always willing to help Scar because she was cute and knew how to charm him. But even he couldn't find Carlo's place. Our only option was the game, but I'd promised Kai I'd take a break from virtual reality until he could join me.

While he took Wendy to school, I ignored the quiet in the house by turning the music up loud. The movie score songs put me in the mood to read, so I grabbed Pinocchio's book. The cartoon version offered nothing helpful, but I flipped through to the end. Scribbles from Wendy's book-coloring phase marked the pages, but the fact that she'd matched the crayon to the color of the fairy's hair impressed me. I slapped the book shut and traded it for my phone where Google would give me more information about the little lady with wings.

I dug through websites that analyzed Carlo Collodi's story of the wooden puppet and discovered that the fairy wasn't supposed to be part of the author's original vision. The editor insisted Collodi add a happy ending after Pinocchio died.

Ebenezer Scrooge. I scrubbed my hand over my face and rubbed at my eyes with the heels of my palms. Why had I forgotten the puppet hung himself in the original story? Thankfully, the editor's demand was the silver lining in the cloud hanging over my head. In the final version, the blue fairy saved Pinocchio's life and grants him life as a real boy.

The front door swung open as Kai carried yet another armful of bags inside. He dropped a plastic bag into my lap with the name of my favorite restaurant splashed on the side. Apparently, he'd noticed my lack of appetite lately and wanted to force-feed me Cheesecake Factory.

"I'll snack after we play," I said, grabbing the headset and easing it over my face.

Two blue lines appeared on the screen. Fortress Clash mocked my inability to get pregnant with its loading lobby. Each player had a unique login lobby tailored to their character's experience. Mr. Geppetto had claimed his character's area was once full of scenery and buttons that, when clicked, revealed pieces of lore on the game's backstory.

I'd march the headset across the room and launch it off our balcony if I didn't desperately need it to save Carlo. Besides, I was starting to like the login sound. The epic song lifted and fell with Game of Thrones-style emotion. It'd taken me a day to create my character, and I only left the lobby to pack Wendy's bag that she took to her grandparent's house. I'd cried when she left, but the game sufficiently distracted me. As soon as I'd put the headset back on, learning the controls kept me so busy I didn't have time to obsess over how my daughter skipped off into her grandma's arm with a dry eye and as little as a hug for mommy.

"Okay, I'm in," Kai's voice echoed from somewhere outside the headset.

"I don't see you."

"You have to get out of the lobby."

I groaned and spun around in the real world to move the character's body. A door, not unlike the portals Scarlet used to create, appeared before me. I reached out and tried to grasp the knob.

My hand passed through the object, so I tried again. It happened again, and I grunted, ready to take a fist to the non-existent door.

"Click the button to interact with objects while you reach for it," Kai said. His voice was distant, muffled as if behind the door or... I didn't want to think about the other option. I'd never seen the fabric of reality torn between the fictional and real worlds, and I didn't want to. Some things should be left to the imagination.

I did as he instructed, clicking the control while reaching for the handle. It worked and the cool feel of the knob sent a chill up my arm. Light flooded the virtual room, causing me to squint as I stepped out of the lobby.

The silhouette of a figure blocked the blinding brightness of the sun that hung over the world of Fortress Clash. My heart skipped a beat at the sheer size of the creature.

It bent forward and reached for my throat. I instinctively leaped back and crashed into the coffee table. My real body lost balance, and I landed on my back on top of the table. A twinge shot up my spine where my tailbone smacked into the edge of the table.

"What's going on?" Kai's echoed voice again but not muffled this time, and deeper than usual.

I straightened the headset and sat up. My eyes had adjusted to the light and the figure vaguely resembled my husband's quirky smile and thick hair. But the similarities ended there. He'd created a character twice his size with shoulders so broad he could balance two milkmaids on either side. The long hair that flowed down his back looked like a rip-off of Fabio and the chain-mail and chest plate placed him in the medieval world.

"Hey, you look the same," he said.

"Yeah," I grunted as I stood and shifted my body forward with a click of the movement button. Combined with my real movements, I got the hang of controlling the character. "I thought it should match me."

"Nah," he said, "the whole point of playing games is getting the chance to be someone different. Do you see these muscles? Look at them!" Kai's character flexed, and the bulge of virtual muscle could have been a mountain.

"If you stop doing so much cardio, you could build muscle too. Also, why do you sound like Morgan Freeman?" I asked, weirded out by all the changes.

"This is fun!" Kai ignored the question and bounded off down the cobblestone street. He waved his meaty hand, beckoning me to follow. "Let's go find the jester."

The image of the barbarian-like figure skipping down the virtual road sent me into a fit of laughter that I quickly coughed under control. Now wasn't the time to enjoy myself. I had a mission, a life to save, a boy to find.

I'd use the hood and do something good for once.

I followed Kai to the armory, where we stocked up on cheap swords that the non-player character shopkeeper warned would break easily. Our accounts didn't have enough coin to purchase the weapons on the tall racks. So we left with the crap swords at our hips.

"Can you feel that?" I asked as we headed for the castle. The hilt of the sword bumped against my leg every time I took a step. I pulled the weapon out and traced my finger along the flat side of the blade. "It's cold."

"This is why we got weapons," he said. "If someone attacks you again, I'll jump him while you take the headset off."

"I can't actually be in the game."

"Why? Johnson was."

I didn't want to think about that. Scar gave up trying to teach me how to create portals because I had never mastered the art. I wasn't Johnson; I wasn't Scarlet—I was merely a mom who'd wanted to protect her daughter from a destiny with death. The result was the transfer of the hood's powers.

I reached to twirl the hood's strings around my fingers. It had become a habit, a sort of security blanket, to remind myself that the hood existed. The strings were the only portion of the fabric that was visible and tangible unless I willed the hood to materialize. If magic like that was possible, it wasn't far-fetched to think I'd literally stepped inside Fortress Clash.

The strings weren't there. I glanced down at my chest, scrambling for the hood. I only wore a plain dress with nothing around my neck. The hood was gone.

My heart pounded, and I tugged at the headset.

"What's wrong?" Kai asked as he opened the massive door to the castle. He let it fall shut and reached for me.

"I can't—the hood, it's gone."

"It's actually…not." My husband's barbarian face twisted in confusion. "I can see it."

"What?"

Kai ran his palm over my shoulder. "I can't feel anything, but it looks soft like the Velveteen Rabbit."

"You can see it?" I hadn't willed the hood to materialize. Somehow, the game showed it without my permission.

Kai nodded. "It looks heavy. Good thing you can't feel it in real life. That'd be a thousand degrees to wear in California summers."

He turned and pulled the door open again. It groaned from the weight of the wood. Another player burst out the other side of the doors and ran for the gate. He wore a mask that reminded me of Batman's villain with the Darth Vader voice. But the Harry Potter scar emerging from behind the mask and disappearing into his hairline wasn't covered. Another character ran after him with his sword drawn. The second character appeared to be a guard of some sort, ready to cut down the player for stealing something from the castle.

"So apparently you can play good side or dark side. As soon as you make a choice that the game considers evil, it places you on the dark side and all the NPCs that are designed for the good side will attack you."

"What the hell is an NPC? Can you just stick with English, please?" I followed him into the dim hallway. Lanterns lined the castle, flickering as if the wind were real. A cool breeze swept down the open hall, stirring dust from between the cracks in the floor.

"NPC is short for non-player characters. The fake people built into the game like Carlo has supposedly become. It saves time to use an acronym."

"Uh-huh, yeah." I rolled my eyes. "We saved a split second speaking in acronyms instead of the real words."

"Talk about real." Kai stopped in his tracks. I bumped into his back and my face hit the rock-hard, rippling muscles under his character's shirt. I reached out to run my hand over the impossible bulges, but Kai swiveled. "Do you see this?" He pointed into the throne room.

Blood covered every surface, splattered like a horror movie across the floor, over the walls, and pooled on the seat of the throne.

"Oh, my—" I gagged. I'd seen plenty of blood and dead bodies before, but actual crime scenes never looked like this. The king's entire family, plus guards and other characters, lay slaughtered in every corner of the room. The chandelier that glittered in the center of the room was dulled with red flecks dotting the sides of the candles. An endless burn of the flame melted wax over the edges of the cups designed to hold the candles, and both blood and wax dripped from the chandelier like a slow, eternal shower of death. "Look for the court jester!" I squealed. Once I gained control of my stomach, I tiptoed around the room, peering at each character's face. We already knew Carlo would look like himself based on Mr. Geppetto's ability to recognize him. But would I recognize him covered in blood and guts?

"Someone definitely chose the dark side." Kai's Adam's apple bobbed as he swallowed. "I don't see any clothing that would resemble a jester. But we need the king to help us find the people who work in his court. So, what do we do now?"

I breathed again, though the smell of iron and the stench of decomposing flesh caused me to dry heave. Carlo was alive. Maybe. I hadn't failed yet.

"Okay, um—" What would I do if this were an actual murder? Where would I take the investigation next? I'd ask witnesses. "We need to find other players who might have seen what happened."

"The guy who ran out!" Kai snapped his fingers.

"Good." I nodded. "Let's find him."

As soon as we made it to the hall, I took a gulp of air. "Can you smell that?"

"You mean the plastic smell from the headsets? I think it will wear off the longer they're out of the packaging."

"Never mind."

The walk along the cobblestone streets felt like it took forever. Players outside the castle didn't have a clue what we were talking about, but one pointed us toward a dark side player last seen entering the tavern.

It didn't take long to find the tavern with the raucous laughter and chanting players, screaming for their favorite in a fistfight outside. We pushed through the doors and the smell of wheat and beef assaulted me. The sensations of the game grew more powerful. The brush of an NPC's body against my back as he pushed through the crowed room nearly knocked me over. Even the slight taste of the mead moistened my tongue.

I ignored it for now. We had a murder investigation to solve. Not an actual murder, of course, but the answer would lead us to a real person.

Mr. Batman Villain Mask stood at the bar, ordering a round of pints for everyone in the room. Of course, he had more than enough coin to spoil the entire tavern with mead after murdering the king.

It's just a game, Mari. Get it together.

But bringing justice to the NPCs of Fortress Clash consumed me and I liked how it felt a lot better than reminders of the hood or my empty womb.

"That's him." I raised my arm and pointed at the man downing a pint. The beverage splashed over his face and beaded on his beard.

"Let's see what this button does," Kai said. His hulking figure barreled through the crowd. Thick fingers wrapped around the masked man's neck, and Kai pinned his body against the edge of the bar. "Huh, that's what that does." He dropped the man but blocked his escape.

"What the—" the player spewed a string of curses.

I shoved past Kai and thrust my finger into the man's face.

"You really think buying the bar a round of crappy drinks is going to pull you from the dark side after you murdered the king and his entire family? Think again, Buster."

"Buster?" Kai wrinkled his nose.

I waved my hand. "I don't know, just go with it."

"You're messing with my game, you psycho—" the player called me a few creative names before my barbarian-sized husband slapped his massive hand over the man's mouth.

"We're looking for someone and the king was supposed to point us toward him," I explained while the character's eyes darted between the tiny woman and her hulk of a husband. "And since you killed the king. I need you to fix this."

Kai released him long enough to allow him to speak. Of course, the nut-bag launched into another string of unrepeatable words that Kai cut off once again. This time with a slap.

A colorful bar appeared over the character's head. The bar was seventy-five percent full of green while red filled in the last section. It blinked and dropped another two percent.

"What's that?" I asked.

"It's my health bar, you idiot," he spat. "Your tank here could have killed me. And they're not reviving characters anymore. I'd have lost this character forever."

"Like the king?"

"He's an NPC. Besides, with all the updates, the game is bugged."

"Bugs?" My skin crawled as if spiders skittered up my arm. Instead, it was just the splash of mead that now dried and left my arm sticky with the little hairs pulling against my skin. "What does that mean?"

"Bugged," he repeated. "The original Fortress Clash is being erased. Supposedly we'll get to keep our characters, but anything we do right now gets wiped. The game doesn't care what you do. I could burn this whole town down and collect the coin. The NPCs aren't storing any new information."

"How long until it's completely erased?" I asked.

The man shrugged and pulled off his mask. The baby-like face underneath shocked me. Why wouldn't this player choose a more menacing-looking character like Kai had? Did he want it to reflect the look of his real-world person like I did?

"Four-ish days," he said. "They started the reset on the servers a long time ago."

"Then what happens?"

After leaning back against the counter, the player snatched the handle of a cup and tossed his head back. Once he slammed the empty cup against the bar top, he burped, and finally acknowledged my question. "Everything is gone. That's why I killed royalty. Rumor is that we keep our equipment and characters, but the rest of the game gets wiped. I can store a bunch of crap and have it carry over after the update with no repercussions."

Another fight broke out behind us. An assassin-styled woman skipped around and swiped her blades at another character whose health bar instantly dropped to ten percent. It blinked wildly, flashing red, until he grabbed a potion from his pouch and downed it. Green filled in half of the health bar.

"It's wild up in here." The masked man laughed. "If you have any loot at all. I suggest getting better swords to protect yourself."

"We just want to find the court jester from the game. Any idea where he'd be?" Kai asked.

The man pursed his lips. "Bunch of players from my guild took royal NPCs hostage, for ransom, from the king. I thought it was a waste of time, so I killed them and took the coin I could find. The stupid guild leader says I could have gotten more from the ransom because it's impossible to find where all the coin is stashed. Some areas of the game are blocked off while they wipe the content and replace it. But NPCs can access them. Whatever. I got plenty." He held up a bag that jingled.

"Where are they holding the NPCs?" I asked.

"NPCs, huh?" Kai craned his meaty neck to look at me. "You're getting into this."

The guy ignored our personal side-conversation. "The dragon cave. The guild caught a specific time when the dragon was bugged and not attacking. They dropped the NPCs there." He took a swig from someone else's drink. I'd have warned him about getting sick like any good mom does when a person over shares but thought better of it. The guy wiped the foam from his upper lip and leaned his elbows on the bar top again. "What do you want with the NPCs, anyway? The gold is in the castle somewhere. You'll barely get any loot from NPCs right now."

"Call it a quest," I said. "If I can find the court jester—" I almost explained that I'd save a real person's life but stopped myself. The guy didn't need to think we'd lost our marbles. We already sucked at the game. "Then I get to do some cool stuff. My character levels, or something, I think."

"Right," he said. "Well, if you're going to face the dragon, you'll need better swords than those." He nodded toward the weapons at our hips.

"How do we get them? The game won't let us buy the expensive ones."

He laughed. "You can't just buy them. You have to trade quests with the weapon smith. The quests will take days. Real days."

I sighed and slumped against the counter. "We don't have days."

"Good luck." He shrugged and turned around. The character behind the bar opened a cabinet that revealed bottles in the colors of the rainbow. It didn't match the surroundings or the rest of the game. One of them had a tag hanging from the cap that read *drink me*.

Where had I seen that before? I shook my head and turned to Kai. I'd never get used to seeing his tiny head on the oversized body.

"Come on, we've got a dragon to fight." I ducked past the assassin player and dipped out the door.

"Nope, no way you should go into the cave without better weapons. You *felt* it when Mr. G's character got stabbed, Mari. What if—"

"We're not going without better weapons." I marched toward the armory, pushing past players raiding an innocent NPC's house. Fortress Clash had officially turned into The Purge. Players went wild with the game's update issues.

"But the dude said it will take days to get enough money to buy them."

"We're not going to buy them," I said with a glance back at my tank of a husband. "We're going to steal them."

Chapter 7

Sticky Fingers

For half a day, I cased the armory. Each time we tried to storm it, NPCs caught us, forcing us back to the street. I tried tricking the weapon smith, but the game still did not allow access beyond the shopkeeper's body.

I asked other players for help but everyone had gone rogue. With the updates about to drop, players scrambled for last-minute loot. One archery woman stopped long enough to tell me how to find my map and where to locate the dragon cave within it. But I still couldn't go there without the right weapons because it'd be a waste of time.

And when you're a mom, a full-time journalist, a wife, and the Keeper, you don't have time to waste.

Not to mention the fact that this week was supposed to be our anniversary vacation. We'd already lost the rest of the day to Kai's attempt at locating the creators of Fortress Clash. Even our combined investigation skills came up with nothing.

I marched up to the armory again, this time with a torch in hand that I'd stolen from the castle hallway. I tossed it inside and waited for the NPCs to evacuate the building. Maybe without the shopkeeper's body in the way, I could squeeze to the back of the room and grab the swords.

Heat licked at my back. I walked forward, but the game stopped me short. An invisible barrier blocked me from stepping within reach of the high-level weapons. I grunted and shoved my real-world body forward. I stumbled, smacking my shin against something, likely the coffee table. In-game, my character's health bar blinked and dropped, leaving me with three percent less green.

"Ouch." I straightened. The flames had caught hold of the dry wooden floor and spread to the back of the room. The burn of fire caused sweat to drip down my temples and pool inside the headset, where the equipment sealed against the skin on my face. I pulled at it but the headset wouldn't budge.

When I tried again, I panicked and let go of the headset. Flames scorched the back of my ankle, sending excruciating pain up my legs. I dance around in the game and swatted at the bottom of the character's dress. The fire was relentless, closing in on me now. I tried to tear the fabric off, but it burned too fast and crawled up the skirt.

"Mari!" A hulking figure appeared past the wall of flames. "Wake up!"

"What?" It sounded like he told me to wake up. But I wasn't asleep. I was playing the game.

"Mari!" my husband's deep voice squealed. That sounded more like my Kai rather than the barbarian character he played.

Smoke gathered in the small building, causing me to choke and cough. I scratched at my throat, trying to feel for the hood and myself.

This isn't real. You've been playing the game too much, and this is just a nightmare. Way to go, Mari.

The searing pain of melting flesh jolted me from the thoughts. I screamed and did the only thing I could think of. I stopped, dropped, and rolled, though there wasn't much space that the fire hadn't consumed.

Instead of putting out the fire, my body shook. The weight of someone's grip took me by the shoulders and yanked my body up and down. I kicked at the invisible attacker. My heart pounded, and I wondered if I'd had too much coffee too late in the day. This nightmare wouldn't give up. The crash of metal sliced through the crackle of flames. One by one, the swords fell from their holding places as the fire ate away at the building.

I flipped onto my stomach and crawled for the weapons. My fingers splayed, trying to reach for the hilt of a high-level sword, but hands dug into my shoulders.

I screamed and twisted, then launched my fist forward, hoping to land it against whoever was holding me back.

"Ow!"

All at once, the flames, the armory, and the high-level sword vanished. My head pounded and the skin on my ankle throbbed so badly it seemed my pulse would push right out of the bonds of my flesh.

Kai lay leaned against the couch with both hands cupping his nose. My headset was in his lap with the wires from the controllers tangled in his legs. Blood dripped from his nostrils as he pulled his fingers back and sat up.

"Are you okay?" he asked.

"What—Ebenezer Scrooge that hurts!" I twisted my leg to see the back of my ankle. Sure enough, the skin bubbled and yellowed from a first-degree burn. My entire calf was painted red and the flesh at the bottom peeled away. I seethed and forced myself to look away before I was tempted to touch it.

"You were just standing there," Kai said between breaths. He wiped at his nose with the back of his wrist, but the blood kept gushing.

"Did I hit you?"

He nodded. "You wouldn't move. It was so freaky, and not the good kind of freaky. You were in a trance or something. Then I tried to take the headset off, but it was on tight and you suddenly started reacting to my touch and kicking me off of you."

I swiped my palm over my forehead to brush wispy, escaped strands of hair from my face. My hairline was slick with sweat and I struggled to catch my breath as realization set in.

Not only did I hurt myself and my husband, I failed to get the swords. And how much longer did we have until Carlo was stuck in the game forever?

"I'm sorry," I said.

Kai leaned forward and gently wrapped his arms around me. "I'm just glad you're okay. That was spooky."

"I'm going to dress this wound and try again." I stood and limped toward the kitchen.

"No, no way," Kai said, following me.

I crouched and reached for the first aid kit under the sink, and Kai copied.

"You're bleeding all over the floor." I pointed to the spots of red everywhere. "Here." I pulled the kit open and gathered the gauze. Kai shoved the white fabric inside his nostrils and followed me back to the couch.

"This is insane. The game hurt you."

The realization of what happened hit me and excitement sent my heartbeat speeding up. If I could use this incident to get to Carlo, a first-degree burn was worth it. "This could help me figure out how to go inside the game the same as Johnson did." With every word, I spoke faster.

"Please don't try it again."

"Kai, Carlo is trapped in there. This is no different from any other case. Someone is in danger, and if I have the information on how to help them, I will." I discarded the first aid kit on the couch cushion and snatched a block of sticky notes from the coffee table. I peeled off three notes and slapped them against the top of the table.

On yellow: *Get weapons, get past the dragon, find Carlo in-game. Ask him for his address.*

On orange: *If he doesn't give it to us, guide Carlo back to his unique login lobby.*

On red: *Use login lobby to locate the IP address and find his real-world body to help him remove the headset.*

On the back of the red note, I scribbled another goal. *Keep eyes peeled for Johnson in the game.*

"Please, just let me try to contact the creators of the game again. They can pause the updates and locate Carlo's account."

"You tried that already." I shot Kai an impatient look. We'd wasted a whole day while he tried to track down the makers of Fortress Clash. Nothing panned out. It was as if they didn't exist.

"Okay, but you can't log back in right now."

"Why not?"

Kai frowned. He pulled the bloody gauze from his nose and sighed. "We're going to miss our appointment."

I swallowed the lump in my throat and shook my head.

Kai opened his mouth to argue, but I interrupted. "Nope. I can't, I just can't do that right now."

"Mari, we've been waiting months to see the specialist."

"So she can tell us I'm infertile? I'm too old? Or maybe the hood is controlling my destiny and making me barren because a Keeper can't be a mom?" My chest heaved as the words spilled out of my mouth. I couldn't stop them any more than Kai could stop the blood dripping from his injured nose. We were a pair. A mess.

I'd seen my husband speechless before, but this wasn't one of those times. His frown softened, and he said nothing as he sat down beside me. The couch cushion sunk under his weight and warmth encircled me as he pulled me into him.

Tears stung my eyes, and it had nothing to do with the pain of my burned ankle. My breath shuddered and fat tears spilled over my eyelids, rolling down my cheeks one by one. The pain of dozens of negative pregnancy tests came rushing back all at once. It dulled the physical throbbing in my leg.

Kai caught the tears on his fingers before they could slide to my chin.

"Just let me save Carlo," I said. "I can do it."

"If you want to stop trying for another baby, just say the word. I'm on board with whatever you want."

I sniffled and sat up, facing my husband. "All I want right now is to get into the game and help Carlo find his way out."

Kai nodded. "Okay, I'll call and reschedule the appointment. Or… cancel?" He pursed his lips.

"Reschedule, that's fine."

"Got it. Will you at least wait for me to get into the game with you so I can help? I can be a meat shield."

I smirked. "Sure. Just hurry." I pulled the headset over my head, but didn't turn it on. The pain in my leg had me hesitating. Would I log in to find myself burning in the armory? Could I fully step into the Fortress Clash? And if so, could I get my body past the invisible barriers that blocked the characters?

I could march right past the shopkeeper and find Carlo much faster without restrictions. We had less than two days to locate him and snag his address before they wiped the game. I worried the content changes had caught up with him and we'd need to use his IP address to find where his internet was coming from. The IP address would give us a location and we'd barge in to rip the headset off just like Kai had done to me. Hopefully, Carlo wouldn't punch us.

"Yes, I'm calling to change our appointment." Kai's voice was muffled by the headset. "No, no reason for congratulations."

My heart cracked.

"It's just a scheduling conflict. Can we come by another time?"

I clicked the button to turn on the headset. The loading screen song drowned out my husband's voice and the rest of the phone call. Orchestral music rose and fell with drama. The closer it got to loading the game, the more intense the rhythm became.

I adjusted the settings to turn the sound up louder. Still, no amount of Game of Thrones-style songs could drown out my thoughts.

You can't bring more life into this world. But you can save Carlo's.

The same thought cycled through my mind over and over until I felt dizzy and light-headed. Or maybe that was the pain of my throbbing flesh. Either way, I didn't have time to stop and analyze it. So, I let the message repeat like a broken record in my brain.

Don't. Mess. This. Up.

Chapter 8

Weathering the Storm

The low-level sword cracked as it whacked against a boar's tusk. The creature lunged at me, knocking me back into Kai's twelve-pack abs. Everything around me flashed red. The bloody color blinked faster and faster until my character's knees buckled. I stumbled, but my husband steadied me after defeating another boar. An ache in my torso throbbed where the boar's tusk jammed into me.

I shrieked and stabbed the broken end of the blade between the animal's eyes.

Speaking of eyes, I squeezed mine shut. I'd said it before and I'd say it again. I wasn't a killer. Not even of villains. Not when I couldn't help it (AKA self-defense with the wolf and all that jazz). So murdering the innocent boar didn't sit well with me and I didn't want to witness it collapse to the ground with blood and brains exposed.

Strong arms wrapped around me. Kai's massive body blocked the cool breeze that bent the tall grass across the meadow. Warmth surrounded me and I felt safe enough to open my eyes.

Instead of a gruesome scene, the animal had vanished. In its place sat a pile of shiny gold coins.

"What the—"

"It's not real," Kai said. His rippling muscles and excessively deep voice reminded me of that, but something about Fortress Clash *felt* real. I couldn't shake it. "You kill the creature, level up, and then we access the swords."

"Right." I nodded and sucked in a deep breath. It was supposed to take days to complete the quests necessary to access the high-level weapons, and I could barely fight one boar.

One failure after another. Shame struck through my heart like a bolt of lightning. I couldn't even play a stupid video game well enough to help Carlo.

"We need a different plan."

Kai nodded. "Especially considering your health bar is dangerously low. Can you…" he paused. "Can you feel that?"

"No," I lied.

Even with the character's face, I could sense my husband's skeptical look. He shook his head and stomped through the grass. "We're going back inside the fortress."

"But the quest—"

"We need a different plan, remember?" When he tapped his nonexistent watch, he was just slapping his bare wrist. The gesture was loud and clear—we were running out of time.

"Okay." I glanced around, using my surroundings to spark an idea. The empty meadow gave me nothing, but I'd worked under pressure before. I could do this. What did I do with real-world investigations? I studied other murders to track killers, I took meticulous notes on the details of the cases, and I worked with detectives, other journalists, and witnesses. An idea struck me harder than the boar's tusk. The game dinged, and a glow appeared above my character's head. Somehow, it knew my thoughts. *Creepy.*

"We need a team. When I work on a case, you help and Detective Wilhelm works with me. And now Scar is my assistant."

"We could get a higher-level player to snag the swords for us?"

I smiled. My husband was a genius with Thor-sized muscles. If we had time for a break, I knew how I'd want to spend it.

"Let's do it."

Back inside the fortress, we stopped the woman with the bow and arrow. She looked like a Lord of the Rings elf with carved archery equipment minus the pointy ears. The name Loxley89 floated above her head. Her health bar nearly quadrupled ours and the pack slung on her back never ran out of arrows.

"Please," I begged. "We need the swords. We will give you everything we have."

"You're both newbie players. What could you have that I'd want?" Loxley89 asked. She folded her arms across her chest. A metal dragon-shaped clip held her auburn hair in a messy bun.

"Ebenezer Scrooge," I cursed. We had nothing to offer. Apparently, five thousand gold coins were nothing in Fortress Clash. I had no idea we'd need so much.

"Skin!" Kai poked his meaty finger into the air.

"Don't be creepy," I said.

"No, we'll gift you skins if you do this for us."

Loxley89 arched her eyebrow. "You're willing to spend real-world money for the basic shopkeeper swords? You know you can just finish the quests and get them, right?"

"We don't have time," he explained. "It's a whole thing with dragons and Pinocchio—"

I waved my hand to cut Kai off before he confused the poor woman. "Tell us how to get the skins and we'll do it."

"Fine," she agreed. "Drop the gift into my account. I won't use it until after the update in case the old skins get wiped. Once I see it, I'll go get your swords."

Loxley89 disappeared into the armory and reappeared only moments later. When she dropped the sword into my hands, I dropped like an anchor. Despite the excessive muscles, Kai did the same. He stumbled forward until he clicked to release his hold on the weapon. It clattered to the cobblestone path.

Loxley89 laughed. "You can store them, but you won't be able to use them. Didn't you know your level has to match the sword's level? Oh, and a barbarian wields an ax which you can only get from the barbarian guild. Unless you're level one hundred, then any character can use any weapon."

"So I'm the only one who can use the swords?" I asked.

"When you level." She nodded and skipped down the path, pausing long enough to whip out an arrow, nock it on the bow, and release. We watched, speechless and frustrated. The arrow dug into a dark side player's face. Unlike the boar, the violence didn't vanish. The player dropped and gushed blood from his temple. Loxley89 looted the body and shot us a wink that reminded us her level was infinitely higher than we'd ever achieve.

We're in way over our heads.

I shook off the thought and pressed forward. When I clicked to store the weapon, my body moved slower. The weight of it pulled against my shoulders and slowed my character's movements, but it'd have to be good enough. When Kai clicked to store the sword, it popped back out, materializing from his pack and dropping to the ground. He tried again, but the process repeated. Kai didn't give up, clicking and clicking as we walked. Eventually, he agreed to abandon the weapon so we could pick up the pace and make it to the cave before the game's sun fell below the horizon.

"I don't like this." Kai groaned. Shadows obscured the mouth of the dragon's cave. "What good is the sword if we can't wield them?"

"Carlo is level bajillion. I'm sure he can use it. We just need to get to him and have him fight the dragon so we can all get out."As I marched toward the entrance, an icy draft swept through the dark corridor and blasted into my face. A low roar rumbled from somewhere deep inside the darkness. Goosebumps prickled over my arms and sent a shiver down my spine. The plan sucked, but it'd have to do.

"Mari…"

"Don't say it." I held up my palm like a valley girl from the nineties. *Talk to the hand.*

"Let me do it," Kai said as he stepped in front of me.

"No, we're not letting your character die." I pushed past him. "You'd have to make a new one, then level enough to hike out here. It would take way too long. I'm the only one who can carry the sword. I'm taking it to Carlo."

"You're stubborn."

"Thank you."

"It wasn't meant as a compliment," he muttered and followed me into the cave. The moment we stepped into the shadows, the temperature dropped. Another rumbling groan swept through the corridor with the smell of smoke. Warm air wrapped around us—the dragon's breath.

"Stubborn. Determined. What's the difference?" I reached for the pack on my back and produced a flaming torch. How it lit straight from the pack, I didn't know, but I didn't care to question the impossibilities of the game.

Flickering light danced along the walls of the cave. Long, ragged scratch marks scarred the floor and walls and red stained the corridor. I ignored the obvious warning signs and focused on the dirt puffing up with our every step. The minor details grounded me and kept me pressing forward. Real or not, it had consumed Carlo, and he needed my help to get out.

The further we traveled inside the cave, the lighter our surroundings became. We stepped from the dark corridor into an open space where the path stopped at a ledge. It dropped into an abyss of coin. A massive red and orange creature lifted its long neck and released sparks that matched its scales.

An ear-splitting roar encompassed us as if the sound itself were tangible. My heart leaped into my throat and blocked all sound as I opened my mouth to scream. Heat from the dragon's breath curled the escaped strands of hair that floated around my face.

Kai shot me a bug-eyed look, and I slapped my hand to my chest as the dragon spoke again, this time with words.

"Only a few find the way," it said. I tossed the torch back into the dark corridor and we dove for a shadow, hoping the dragon couldn't see us under the outcrop of rock.

The creature's mouth twisted into a chilling grin. Red and orange flickered, changing to brown and white. The spikes on the dragon's back disappeared and fur replaced it. The only thing that remained the same was the white fangs in its jaw.

"Some don't recognize it and when they do, they don't want to."

In a flash, the creature returned to its original shape and color. The dragon reared its head back, and the grin vanished.

Where did I hear that quote?

I knew those words. I'd seen them or read them on a billboard or book or news article. And why did the dragon have fur? All the clues added up, but the puzzle didn't have a picture in my mind yet.

I couldn't place the quote, but I spied movement behind the beast. On the other side of the ledge that circled the pit, the shape of a body wriggled and squirmed. I squinted and caught sight of a familiar fuzzy head.

"It's Carlo." I breathed.

"Mari!" Kai screamed, shocking me back to reality—not reality.

The dragon had spotted us. Its eye squelched and a layer of film rolled back as it fixed its gaze on us. Before I could think, claws ten times the size of my body slashed at me.

Kai yanked me out of the way, and the dragon's claw dug into the rock. Pieces of the wall and ledge broke off into pebbles and larger stones that crashed down into the pit of treasure. We scrambled into the corridor, letting the shadow obscure us from the dragon's searching eye.

"We have to get to the other side," I said.

"Oh, hell no."

Before Kai could stop me, I grabbed the torch from the dusty floor and launched it into the pit. The dragon roared, and followed the object with its gaze.

I darted to the ledge, skipping over the fallen rocks.

"Mari!" Kai whispered.

The dragon slashed at the torch, extinguishing it. It roared and flickered to a furry creature that resembled a cat again. The glitch gave me enough time to side-step along the ledge. The dragon grabbed at the torch again until it sunk into the coins. Millions of gold coins spilled and sunk as the beast adjusted its weight on the treasure and buried the torch.

Carlo scooted from the shadow long enough for me to spot him.

Pure fear twisted his face from the nerdy, intelligent young man I'd seen deliver our DoorDash orders to a child living in a nightmare.

"Help me," he mouthed the words, but he didn't risk putting voice to them. Desperation had changed him, but a glimmer of hope in his face inspired me to say something—anything to calm him.

"I have the dragon sword," I said, pointing to my pack. I'd acted impulsively, wanting to comfort the poor boy. Instead, I'd alerted the dragon with my voice. My heart pounded until it threatened to leap from my chest and plummet into the pit to be buried with the torch.

The dragon whipped its head around and Carlo scrambled back into the darkness. The creature's mouth curled into another grin that struck me as familiar. Where had I seen that twisted smile before?

Like with a case, the clues rushed at me all at once. The *drink me* tag in the tavern, the grin, and the NPCs that looked like a deck of cards added up to a classic story.

"It's Alice in Wonderland!" I squealed. The epiphany spilled from my mouth before logic in the face of danger could save me.

The cat-dragon flickered, and it roared. Fiery breath caused me to cough and sputter as smoke filled the surrounding air. The beast swiped claws bigger than my entire body at the ledge, but it missed when Kai shouted at it from the other side of the pit.

"Over here!" He'd produced the torch from his pack and waved it around.

The dragon wasn't amused or easily distracted. It only glanced at my husband before it reared back and prepared a scaly arm to slash at me again.

I froze, unable to move, but my mind still worked. Kai had said he could see the hood, which meant it was still there, in the virtual world. I willed it to materialize. If the dragon could hurt my real body, that meant the hood could protect me, too.

Blood red velvet fabric filled in over my shoulders with the hood folded down my back. The claws came down again and blinding fear rippled through me.

I clung to the clues I'd solved and silenced the scream within me, forming words instead. I scrabbled for the edge of the hood and yanked it across my chest, using the fabric to block me.

"Ask it where to go," I yelled.

It was too late.

The dragon's hand smashed into me with the claw extended and the impact knocking every bit of breath from my lungs. The claw should have sliced me open, but the last thing I remembered was the crunch of bone.

I ripped at the headset. It fell to the floor of our living room and I collapsed.

Pain radiated through my chest as I dropped to my knees. The skin on my legs burned against the rug as I doubled forward and cupped my chest where a rib had surely cracked.

Why had the hood only halfway protected me?

It was the last thought I had managed before the darkness at the corners of my vision filled in and everything went black.

Chapter 9

Out of the Woods

A doctor stood over me with a sheet blocking most of my view of him, but I recognized his features as the face of our elderly neighbor. He tugged and pulled at my midsection. It didn't hurt. Instead, I felt the movement of his fingers inside my belly and registered nothing else until a squeaky cry filled the room.

Kai beamed beside me. He grabbed my hand and squeezed.

"It's a boy!" Somebody said.

"Am I having a cesarean?" I asked, but my mouth filled with cotton, and the words jumbled.

Pain rippled through my torso, and I blinked. The sheet and the baby's cry vanished. Kai and the doctor were the only ones left from the dream. He held my hand, but I laid on our living room couch instead of on an operating table.

Mr. Geppetto stood next to my husband, and he gently pressed his hand on my chest.

"It doesn't appear to be broken," he said. "Likely a nasty bruise to the bone, though."

"Thank you," Kai said with a breath of relief.

"My skills as a medic haven't been used since Vietnam, so I recommend you get a professional doctor's opinion."

Kai nodded.

"What happened?" I asked.

"You fainted. Probably from the pain and the shock of the attack."

I hurried to sit up, but the ache in my ribcage caused me to ease back into the cushion. "What happened to Carlo? Why are you out of the game? We have to go back. I didn't help him. I need to—" The words tumbled out of me, crashing into one another until I barely made sense. Tears stung my eyes as Carlo's desperate expression materialized in my mind. The boy needed me and I'd failed, leaving him in a dragon's pit.

"Your character's health bar dropped to critical," he said with a glance at Mr. Geppetto. "You might have died."

I shook my head. "No, the mourning period—"

Kai nodded apologetically.

"What about Carlo?" *I got him killed, didn't I? Don't say it. Don't say it.*

"When you were attacked, your character dropped everything. He got the sword and cut off the dragon's hand long enough to get around the ledge. But the game glitched. The changes are erasing some of the characters' progress."

My breath hitched. The sad expression on my husband's face told me more than I wanted to know.

"The dragon started over as whole again and repeated what it'd said when we first found it."

"And Carlo?" I frowned. We barely knew the guy, but the thought of him hurt struck me harder than the dragon's attack. He was old enough to be my younger brother if I'd had one, but I saw him as a kid, like Scar—confused, displaced in the real world, and in need of my guidance. The latter was something Wendy slowly needed less and less of, which worked out perfectly since I could pour my energy into Pinocchio.

He still needed me.

"He went back into the shadows where the dragon can't see him."

I perked up and my body followed suit. As I pulled myself to sit upright, I ignored the ache in my ribcage.

"We can go back in. I know what to do."

Kai's brow pinched, and he exchanged a look at Mr. Geppetto. The old man shrugged, and they turned their skeptical gazes to me.

"I don't know how or why, but the game is *Alice's Adventures in Wonderland*."

Kai cringed and gently laid his hand on top of mine. The gesture told me he didn't believe me. "Maybe this isn't another, you know, *Keeper* thing."

"No, I'm not—" I shook my head. "I'm not saying that it is. There's no story aura around the game, but the dragon is the Cheshire cat. It said the same thing the character does in the book. I've been studying the classics. I know it well." The leaning pile of books stacked between the couch and side chair was within reach. I pulled out *Alice's Adventures in Wonderland* from the middle like this was a game of Jenga. After flipping through the pages, I pointed to the illustrations of the Cheshire cat and skimmed the conversation between him and Alice.

"Mari…"

"Actually," Mr. Geppetto interrupted, "what she says makes sense. Game creators have overlain new designs on old games. Fortress Clash was accused of stealing content in the past, but since the creators of the game are anonymous, the accusation went nowhere."

I smiled. I couldn't help it. Whenever clues came together and created a picture, my brain dropped a hit of dopamine. Solving a case would never get old and the entire purpose was to help people.

I slid off the couch and to my knees, reaching over the coffee table for the headset. "I don't think we have to fight the dragon at all. We can talk to it."

"I still can't log in," Mr. Geppetto said. "You kids have fun."

He still thought it was just a game. Or maybe he wanted to ignore the oddities surrounding the situation because he still believed he was losing his marbles. Either way, he hurried to leave our house and get away from the discomfort of it all.

I said goodbye, then pulled the headset on.

"Mari." Kai's voice muffled.

"We're so close, Kai. I'm not giving up now."

I heard him sigh, then the login song drowned him out. The loading screen blinked away and dropped me into the game. Health bar warnings flashed around me, tinting the entire world red.

The dragon's roar exploded until my ears rang like they did at the rock concerts Kai and I used to attend before Wendy came along.

I crawled away from the edge of the ledge and propped myself against the rock wall.

Kai's character dropped back into the game by the corridor. The dragon smashed its giant tail against the pit's wall and jostled us. Kai stumbled forward and tumbled off the ledge. His lugging body didn't have an ounce of grace or balance, but strength saved him.

My breath caught in my throat at the sight of my husband dangling from the ledge.

It's just a game. It's just a game. For him.

My ribcage still ached and the back of my leg throbbed from the burn, but I ignored the reality of the virtual situation.

"Hey!" I screamed and waved my arms. "Over here!"

The dragon whipped its long neck around while Kai scrambled over the ledge and pulled himself back up. Smoke billowed in my face. The creature readied to repeat the attack from earlier, an attack that would surely drop the last bit of my health bar to zero. I coughed and cleared my throat.

"Will you tell me which way I ought to go from here?" Quoting the book was easier than I'd expected.

I held my breath as the creature paused mid-attack. My heart thundered hard enough to worsen the ache in my ribcage. The dragon's claw dropped back into the pit of coins.

"That depends a good deal on where you want to go," it said. The snout split into a grin.

Carlo emerged from the shadows and I side-eyed him. I tipped my head into a slight nod, and he understood. He stepped to the side, stretching to his full height from out of the darkness. The dragon snapped its neck and fixed its sharp gaze on him.

"I don't care!" I hurried to speak Alice's part of the conversation.

The dragon didn't react, so I wracked my brain to recall the conversation between Alice and the Cheshire cat.

"I don't much care where," I repeated.

The slow turn of the dragon's head reminded me of a horror film. "Then it doesn't matter which way you go."

Carlo ran for me and then stooped to pick me up. The boy I was trying to save now had to save me. He had to side-step along the narrow ledge of rock while balancing me in his arms.

The dragon roared, and heat from a spark of flame scorched the rock above us.

Keep talking.

"So long as I get somewhere," I said.

"Oh, you're sure to do that," the dragon responded.

Carlo huffed and puffed, struggling to carry me and keep his balance along the ledge. Kai met us halfway, and they traded. My husband carried me while Carlo lifted the torch.

The dragon's purr echoed behind us as we slipped into the shadows of the corridor with only the torch's flicker to light the way. The glow of the flame danced along the walls and guided us toward the entrance.

"If only you walk long enough," the creature's voice carried through the darkness. We followed Carlo and the flame in his hand. It had me feeling like Frodo, dashing through Mordor under the watchful eye of the Sauron.

And like Frodo, we'd made it.

Why didn't I study books sooner? Books saved lives.

We burst from the cave and into the glow of the world's moonlight. Night had fallen in Fortress Clash, putting the time at T-Minus not-enough-hours until the game wiped and erased Carlo's consciousness forever.

We needed to get Pinocchio a body, STAT.

Chapter 10

Lost at Sea

The trees, the path, and the map were unrecognizable. It looked like Wendy had taken one of those big, pink erasers to the game and scrubbed until the paper ripped. We stood outside the cave, the same cave we'd entered only an hour ago. Did I somehow learn how to teleport us to another location?

Of course not. I couldn't so much as save Carlo, a simple character from a simple, non-violent, gentle story of adventure and identity, much less create portals.

Kai knelt and allowed me to stand, but my knees shook beneath me. Dirt puffed up around me as I folded my legs and sat on the ground while the men caught their breath.

"Thank you." Carlo's gaze bounced between me and Kai. "I don't know how to repay you. My memory is all messed up, and I'd totally forgotten I designed the original skeleton of this game. It was based on my mom's favorite story."

"Alice's Adventures in Wonderland," I said.

"That's right!" Carlo smiled.

"We're not out of the woods yet," Kai said.

Carlo nodded and brushed his palm over the fuzzy peach of his scalp. The buzzed hair barely covered his skull, and the moonlight shined off the sweat beneath. "I know. I can't log out."

"How long has it been?" I asked.

Carlo pulled a small timekeeping device from his pack that produced a digital clock that floated above us in the sky.

He sighed. "Two years."

I exchanged a glance with Kai. The pressed brows told me we'd come to the same conclusion. *Are you thinking what I'm thinking?* Carlo's body should have died of dehydration, malnourishment, and more.

"The story aura," I answered the unspoken question. "It's kept him alive." I shifted my gaze to the half-wooden boy. "How did you get out of the game? We saw your body cause a car accident in San Francisco."

"I didn't get out of the game." The look of confusion on his face matched the squeak in his voice. Carlo had no clue what we were talking about. Did this relate to the game's erased content too? How had that version of him existed in the real world? It wasn't a simulation since it physically smashed the front of the car that had hit him, but it wasn't real either, considering he'd disappeared.

The clock ticked to the next hour, and a strange movement caught my eye. The curve of Carlo's elbow ticked to a perfect right angle. I hadn't noticed the lines in his flesh before. Instead of skin, his body had a splintered look to it like a crudely carved log.

"What's happening?" I pointed to his arm.

Carlo frowned. When he turned his head, the movement was jerky and awkward, unlike a real person. The same deer-in-the-headlights expression covered his face, and he looked like the boy trapped behind a dragon again.

"I don't know," he admitted. "My skin started getting all crusty and my joints wouldn't move well. Doctors couldn't explain it and my health insurance sucked, so I stopped trying to get answers. The only time I felt normal was in the game."

"That makes no sense." I struggled to my feet. The health bar still blinked over my head and the world was tinted red like a cruel reminder of the hood—the article of clothing that haunted me. It had dragged me into the responsibility of the Keeper and forced me to do its bidding, which meant stripping innocent people of their free will. My stomach twisted and knotted, sending bile into my throat. I coughed and gagged until I swallowed the sickly feeling back down enough to ignore it. But my health bar didn't. It dropped twenty percent and the entire world flashed a bright, blinding red.

"We need to get you back inside the fortress and heal your character." Kai's voice trailed at the last word.

I waved my hand to brush off the urgency, because Carlo needed help more than I did. "The story of Pinocchio starts out with him as a wooden boy and he eventually gets a real body. I don't know what this is." My eyes raked over the odd sight in front of us. The poor young man looked stiff, uncomfortable, possibly in pain. No wonder he'd run off into the virtual world to hide.

"Pinocchio?" Carlo's brow knitted, and he flinched when he tilted his head.

"There's no time to explain. Let's get you both to the fortress and log out." My husband pulled out the map and traced his finger along the path until it broke off into a blank area.

"Carlo." I bit my lip and paused, knowing the answer wouldn't be good. The map was a hint, a piece of the problem with the rest of the game. "Can you tell us where you live in the real world? Your address? We need to take the headset off of you."

He shook his head and the timber of his neck creaked and splintered. He flinched again, likely from the pain. "The only thing I remember beyond creating this game was my condition." Carlo raised his arm to highlight that his arm had nearly turned into lumber. "I couldn't stop thinking about it."

"We need to find your body. Are you sure you can't remember anything? Are you living in San Francisco? Did you have a house or apartment?" I asked the important questions, the leading questions that would guide us to answers the way I did as a journalist on a murder investigation. But Carlo didn't have information.

The half-blank, half-sad stare in his eyes sent a shudder through my shoulders. I shook it off. That would never happen to me. I didn't get addicted to video games.

"What happened?" Kai turned the map in every direction, twisting his arms and tilting his head to get a better look. The distraction came as a welcome relief for the young man. Carlo sidled up to my husband and peered at the map.

"I've spent hours upon hours in the game," Carlo said. "I used to know every corner of the map. This isn't Fortress Clash anymore."

I frowned. The updates had caught up with us.

"Don't we have to get to the Fortress to locate Carlo's unique login lobby?" I asked. The fact that I even knew what that meant made me a little proud. I was learning, like an old dog picking up new tricks. Never did I expect to enjoy existing inside a virtual world when real life had plenty of excitement to offer. But here, I could use my knowledge to control things just like I had with the Cheshire dragon.

The little boost of morale paused the flash of red and my health bar ticked up one notch.

"Yes." Kai nodded and folded the map back into his pack. "The login lobby will have his IP address and we can locate where he is in the real world."

"So let's just trace our steps from when we came here."

We stared at the path ahead where trees reached their long, jagged branches down as if to grab at passersby. Darkness cut off our view of what lay beyond, where the map showed nothingness.

"We came from that direction." Kai pointed.

I shook my head. "No, I think it was through the meadow. I remember being in a meadow with a wolf."

"It was a boar, and that wasn't when we came to the mountain."

"This is a cave." I pointed at the yawning opening in the rock behind us.

"Is it?" Kai raised his eyebrows. I turned to follow his gaze and where the shadows of the entrance once were, a ledge dropped off into the darkness. I scrambled away from the edge and watched as dirt and pebbles tumbled over the ledge and vanished, erased forever with the content.

"It's time to go."

The men nodded in agreement. This was our common goal: get to the fortress, snag Carlo's info, and log out.

The forty hours we had left felt like walls closing in. It was enough time to explore the map and make it back. We had wiggle room to make a few mistakes as long as we didn't walk off a ledge and fall into nothing with the areas of wiped content.

The first path came to a dead-end—literally. An NPC's body was twisted and mangled on the ground before us. Dirt covered his limbs and blood stained his clothes. It looked as though he'd tried to crawl away from his attacker with arms outstretched and stomach against the dirt. Whoever had killed him looted everything except the clothes on his back.

"Don't look." I blocked Carlo's view of the bloodshed.

"Um," Kai's voice trailed off.

I spun around to see the source of his confusion. The NPC and his body were gone. The darkness crawled along the ground, spreading slowly like black, poisonous liquid. I gasped and backed up, bumping into Carlo, whose skin poked mine. The timber of his arm scraped against my flesh and left me with several splinters that stuck out at every angle. I yelped and danced sideways to avoid him.

"Sorry," he said.

"Guys, we need to run," Kai interrupted.

The darkness continued its relentless, ominous spread, licking toward our feet. It threatened to swallow us into the blank areas of the map. We turned and hurried for the nonexistent cave. The ledges pulled toward one another, trapping us in between.

"This way!" Kai headed for the forest off the path.

After what felt like hours, we emerged from the trees into an open area. My leg throbbed and the ache in my feet rivaled the pain in my ribcage. With the darkness behind us and no ledges nearby, we allowed ourselves to collapse in the tall grass. The meadow looked vaguely familiar.

"Is this where we fought the wolf to get the ax money?" I asked.

Kai shook his head. "It was a boar, and we bought a sword."

"No, I'm pretty sure it was an ax."

"Sword."

I shot my husband a sharp look. "Ax."

"Does it matter?" Carlo cut in to drop a truth bomb. It didn't matter, but the recognizable area might. We needed to identify our location in order to save time now that we'd escaped the darkness. He stood, the wood in his legs creaking and splintering. It sounded as painful as it looked and I turned away, not wanting to see how closely he resembled the puppet in the old story's drawings.

Would he turn into a marionette and remain immortal? If the story was told backward, how did that affect the aura and the cycle? The more I tried to understand it, the less sense everything made. This was the opposite of how most investigations went. I'd gather clues, speak with people involved, and put the pieces together until the puzzle created a picture.

This picture was upside down, missing pieces, and backward. I rubbed my temples. Maybe the headset was on too tightly.

"What if you log out?" I rested my hand on the bulge of muscle in Kai's forearm. "Look up the maps to the game and tell us how to get back to the fortress while I keep an eye on Carlo."

"And who will keep an eye on you?" Kai shook his head. "Besides, I can't reach my login lobby either."

"Then pull the headset off."

"It's too risky with the content getting erased. If I log out, this location might get wiped and I'll be forced back to my login lobby with no way to find you guys."

"But we have to try something different," I said. "We can't remember where to go. This isn't working and time is running out." The sun peered over the horizon, casting the new day's glow across the meadow. It illuminated the far reaches of the field. Bright colors clashed with the muted browns and greens of the game. Beyond the tall grass, a table sat in the center of a clearing. Decadent desserts covered the table and two chairs were at opposite ends of the long piece of furniture that matched Carlo's timber skin.

"I've seen this before." I stood and walked toward it. The grass brushed over my bare arms and made me itchy. "But I can't remember where." Beyond the clearing, a distant spire pointed into the air, standing taller than the trees. I squinted to make out the shape of the top of the castle. "Look." I glanced back at the men with a smile on my face. Darkness had chased us, Carlo was turning into wood, and I kept getting confused about the details of the game, but this was a ray of sunshine. "It's a shortcut to the fortress!"

Kai followed, hurrying to get ahead of me in case any booby traps might pop up from the ground. His character's progression halted, but his legs continued moving as if he ran in place. An invisible barrier stopped him from going any closer to the table. He tried to reach out, but the game blocked his hand from moving past a certain point.

Slowly, a white iron fence materialized around the clearing like that of a delicate gate protecting a secret garden. The iron burned with a faint glow. If the illumination wasn't colorless, it could have rivaled the glimmer of story aura. It looked vaguely familiar, but I couldn't recall an iron fence or intricately structured gates that formed a triangle from Alice's story. This was something entirely alien.

It kept getting weirder when it allowed me to walk straight into the fenced area. An intense pressure beat down on my body from every direction, and I struggled to take a breath. The air was so thick it stuck in my throat like jelly. I doubled back until the pressure lifted, right at the line that had stopped Kai.

"Open the gate and try walking in," I said. "It's hard to breathe, but we can make a run through to the gate on the other side."

The barbarian's face wrinkled. "What gate?"

"You can't see that?" I put my hands on my hips and gave him a little spice of attitude. "Now who's not seeing what's right in front of their face?"

"The darkness is coming," Carlo shouted.

We both whipped around to see the tick of the hour turn Carlo closer to a puppet. Faint strings hung from his shoulders like spider webs. Slow, rolling darkness crawled along the horizon, eating up the game's sunlight and all the content behind us.

"We're trapped," I breathed.

"Leave," Carlo said. "Take off your headsets."

"No, we came here to get you out."

"Mari, what if hurts you somehow?" Kai asked. "Don't be a hero."

"I have the hood," I said. "I can't die, remember?" *I think.* I couldn't be sure what the hood did for me in the virtual world. It had blocked the Cheshire dragon's full attack, but I'd still gotten injured. It made zero sense.

"We don't know for sure, and I'm not letting you put yourself at risk."

"Kai." I grabbed my husband's arms and forced him to look at me. "Take off your headset and find an answer to this glitch. You're Mr. Research. I know you can figure out how to get him through."

"No."

"Why won't you leave Fortress Clash? What's really going on?" Kai ran his warm hands over my bare arms, soothing me with touch. But disasters like me didn't deserve comfort, not to mention we didn't have time. "Does this have to do with the fertility specialist appointment?"

"A person's life is at stake!" I squealed and threw my arms in Carlo's general direction, pulling away from my husband. His arms dropped like fallen tree trunks at his sides. The sheer size of my husband's character dwarfed both of us. Maybe that was what had stopped him at the barrier.

"The story aura will keep him alive, you said so yourself." He glanced at Carlo.

"Maybe." My foot tapped without my permission as impatience seeped out of me.

"And maybe the game will hurt you."

"I hate to interrupt, but… guys…" Carlo stepped closer to us.

When we turned, I expected to see the darkness reaching its long black fingers toward our feet. Our argument had lost precious moments. I'd lost my focus.

Ebenezer Scrooge, you screwed up again, Mari.

But the content wipe paused and the ledge that dropped off into nothingness stopped several yards away.

"The updates seem to come in waves," he said. "Probably so they can keep the same basic structure of the game."

"Perfect." I faced Kai. "Now you can leave."

My husband's jaw bulged as he gritted his teeth. An exhausted breath escaped him in a huff. "Fine."

He shook his head and curled his bottom lip under. The look of pure frustration, touched with anger and riddled with fear, wasn't one I'd seen on my husband often. Kai was a history buff, a nerd, a runner, a good father, a great role-player, and patient as all hell. But today, right now, in this virtual world, I'd officially pissed him off. Thankfully, this wasn't his normal face, similar but not the same, so I could ignore it for now.

The barbarian character froze for a moment before vanishing from the field.

"Okay, if you can move past the fence, we can try to make a run for it."

Carlo glanced between me and the table. "I can try, but it's never worked before. I know this game, and this area is restricted. Only one player has ever been able to go into the clearing and gamers have speculated that he's the creator of the game. And you, I guess."

Before I could dig for details, Carlo stepped forward, ready to move into the restricted area. A hulking figure materialized and towered over him, casting a shadow twice along the side of the wooden man.

It had only been a minute or two since Kai left the game. His character returned with a curious expression, eyes sweeping over the odd view of nothingness in one direction, a clearing with a dessert and tea table in the other, and a forest beyond. Did the game wipe his character's memory?

"There's no way you found the answer that fast."

The barbarian flicked his eyes toward me. "I've a feeling I'm not in Kansas anymore."

I was ready to battle it out with him again. Kai researched fast while I was the organized, meticulous, and detailed-focused one. But the quote from the famous film threw me off guard.

"Uh…"

"Ooh, you're wooden-y." He raked his eyes over Carlo and arched an eyebrow. Despite my waving hand, his gaze lingered on Carlo. "You've changed a lot since I used you to track Red Riding Hood. And I don't just mean the Pinocchio skin." The barbarian popped his hip out and leaned to one side, biting his bottom lip.

"What. Is. Happening?" I choked out the words.

"Eh, you can't handle the truth." He shrugged, finally breaking his admiring gaze from Carlo.

Realization dawned. Who else spoke in pop culture quotes?

"Scarlet?" I tilted my head.

The barbarian licked his lips and folded his arms across his chest. "Hmm. Bond. Scarlet Bond."

I palmed my face as I shook my head. "That's not your last name."

"I don't have a real last name. It could be my last name. You don't know. Kind of like you don't know how to create portals, you didn't realize that Carlo was actually Johnson, *and* you took the hood off, which will open the gates of story monster hell next century."

I threw up my hands in surrender. "I got it! I suck—wait, Carlo is who?" My bugged eyes flicked from the half-wooden man to my friend wearing my husband's character's skin. What Scarlet said scrambled my brain. We'd been hoping to use Carlo to find Johnson for the past two years, but her claim was like a bucket of ice water dumping over my head.

"Portals, Mari. Portals." She snapped her meaty fingers in my face.

I shook my head. Someday, maybe, possibly, hopefully, my nutty assistant and best friend would learn to speak without cryptic words. Even if she'd found a nice guy on one of her many dates, she'd likely alienate him with movie quotes and every other sentence as a piece of a puzzle. Poor guy wouldn't know what'd hit him.

Another hour must have ticked because Carlo's skin stiffened and splintered. The crack of split wood cut through the silence like a chopped tree falling in the forest. His joints hardened and his fingers stuck out straight. Scar gasped and slapped her palm over her mouth.

"Are you okay?" I reached out to touch him but pulled my hand back after feeling the rough timber of his arm.

"I think so." It was an obvious lie, but Carlo managed a faint smile.

"Kai sent me here because he thought you might listen to me." The words tumbled out of Scar faster than my brain could catch up. "But I also have answers. I used the skills I've been learning as an investigator's assistant—"

"Investigative journalist's intern."

"Elementary, my dear Watson." She waved her hand. "I watched the video of the car accident over and over because I knew something about the body's disappearance was familiar. Then I realized he stepped through a portal. There's no other explanation, and since Pinocchio here can't do that, it had to be Johnson. The process of elimination helped me solve it, just like you taught me. The only thing I've yet to figure out is what story aura he used on the city street but I assumed its like you always say: *another problem for another time.*" Though it was my husband's character's face, I could perfectly picture Scar's red lips curling into a beaming smile. She'd really come into her own as a researcher. How did I not notice that in the video? Why didn't I think of it? And why did he look like Carlo?

I'd really been off my game.

Or *in* a game.

"But wait, I can step into the area. And you—" I pointed at Carlo. "You said only one other player has ever done that before and survived. What was his in-game name?"

"He doesn't have a name. Or stats, or a health bar." Carlo shrugged. "That's why gamers think he's the CEO of the company that bought out Fortress Clash."

The lack of a health bar and name meant this player was actually inside the virtual world—like me. Of course, I existed in both Fortress Clash and in San Francisco, halfway between game and reality. And who else was similar to me?

I groaned. "Johnson creates portals and I'm supposed to do the same. Ebenezer Scrooge…"

Scarlet seethed while my jaw dropped. The three of us stared at the table of brightly colored cupcakes, teacups, and scones, a strange sight in the dark medieval world of Fortress Clash.

I didn't want to say it aloud. I couldn't acknowledge that the only way to save Carlo was an impossible feat I'd never accomplish—another failure on my checklist of crap.

But the words came out, anyway. "It's a portal, isn't it?"

Chapter 11

It's Rocket Science

Let the games begin. Technically, the game had begun as soon as I'd secured the headset over my eyes and clicked the log-in button. The lobby would play my unique character's music that sounded like a mix between the X-Files whistling theme and the drums of a Viking rock band. It was odd, which suited me just fine.

Of course, it'd been a while since I heard the lobby music because, even if I logged out, the game would drop me back where I left off. We'd come so close, yet so far, trapped now between nonexistence and the portal section that restricted players from entering.

While Scarlet chatted with Carlo to keep his mind off of the impending doom, I tested as many theories about the portal as I could think of. Entering the restricted area suffocated me, but the more I tried, the longer I lasted each time.

Scarlet spoke of the silly customers Carlo used to encounter when delivering mobile food orders. Apparently, she'd accompanied him to several locations. She laughed over a memory where an old man answered the door, buck naked and entirely clueless about his state of inappropriate attire. The cluelessness matched Carlo's expression as he listened with a slight tilt of his head like a confused puppy.

Scarlet's laugh faded. "Well, I guess you don't remember…" Her voice became muffled and distant as I pushed through the barrier.

Like an underwater dive, I'd suck in a huge storage of breath and release it in little bubbles as I made my way through the pressure. I could hear nothing except the beat of my heart drumming in my ears. Perhaps the Viking rock genre made sense for me.

I pushed through the pressure chamber and reached the tea party for the first time.

I ran my hand along the edge of the wooden table. It felt nothing like the timber of Carlo's skin. Instead, it was smooth, cold even, more like a metal than lumber. Brightly colored desserts had my stomach growling, but the decadence kept me from tucking a cupcake or cookie into my pocket. Not to mention I hadn't had an appetite in days.

A bit of breath escaped me as I looked up. I wanted to snatch it back and save it to stay at the tea party longer, but it was too late. My storage tank of air dropped a notch and the health bar ticked.

An unmoving NPC stood with one hand brushing the leaves of a bush from her way and the other holding an open book. The familiar sky-blue dress and straw-colored hair identified her as Alice. Frozen, she stared at nothing at the edges of tea time. She'd never made it to the party, or perhaps the game was designed this way.

The silence of the tea party spooked me. Alice looked like an animatronic character in an abandoned amusement park. The sadness of the scene struck me, too, though she didn't look disappointed.

After what looked like a flash of light from the book, I blinked to adjust my eyes. The light flickered again, and I squinted. The book wasn't what it seemed.

I approached Alice, stepping carefully, as if landmines would explode beneath my feet. I trusted nothing about the game—not with the map vanishing before our eyes and the restricted area so heavy. After I released another bubble, I pushed through the pressure and made it within arm's reach of the creepy NPC. As I drew closer, Alice spoke and my heart skipped a beat.

"Hello, welcome to Wonderland. Enter."

A shiver trickled through me. I could hear her voice, but her mouth didn't move and her eyes blinked, staring at nothing. The lack of inter-action and fluid movements distinguished her from the other non-player characters I'd seen. She didn't have a name above her head or a health bar and though I stood close enough to interact with her, she never looked at me. The only movement she could do was a pattern of turning her head to the side, then back to the front when she spoke. The pattern repeated over and over.

A flicker of light caught my eye and bold letters on the surface of the book. They followed a familiar pattern Q W E R T Y. The book wasn't a book at all, but a keyboard—at least on the left page.

"Hello, welcome to Wonderland. Enter." Alice repeated the phrase in a monotone voice.

My finger hovered over the Escape button that blinked a rhythmic light. The bruise on my rib throbbed as my heart pounded against the cage of bones that held my organs inside. I quickly moved my finger and tapped the Enter button, as suggested by Alice.

A screen lit up on the right side of the book with large letters.

Access

Location

In

Computer

Enterprise

What in the Star Trek-spaceship-hell does that mean? That was when I noticed what the line of words spelled.

ALICE.

My lungs squeezed until my surroundings blinked red. The health bar sent me a warning that I'd suffocate if I didn't move out of the restricted area soon. My pulse picked up as I pushed through the thick, unbreathable air. In my rush, I knocked my knee against the table but didn't slow down. The slow-motion run felt like a bad dream and the harder I pushed, the slower I went.

The tightening in my chest reminded me this wasn't a nightmare. I reached for the headset just in case I couldn't make it out in time. Was my real body not breathing, either? The thought struck me like a bolt of lightning.

I could see Scarlet and Carlo on the other side. Scarlet laughed and landed her hand on his arm.

Everything deepened to a bolder shade of red. My dropping health bar tinted the world and block spots dotted my vision. I pushed one foot in front of the other. Carlo glanced my direction then jolted to his feet as fast as his nearly wooden limbs could move. Scarlet followed, and they banged on the barrier. Their mouths opened in silent shouts, silent to me, anyway.

I can't die. I'm immortal. I can't die. I'm immortal.

I chanted the unsure mantra until my brain could no longer focus. The game had already proved it could hurt me—the hood didn't work here, not entirely.

Instead of the darkness in the game's updates, it was my consciousness turning black. I collapsed in the tall grass past the barrier. Scarlet caught me during the fall. Free from the restricted area, I gulped and gasped for breath as fast as my body would allow.

I slapped my hand to my chest to feel the steady rise and fall of my breathing. The rhythm simultaneously soothed and unsettled me. The blinking Escape button materialized in my mind's eye.

"Does an access enterprise location mean anything to you?" I asked Carlo.

Recognition lightened his dark eyes, and a faint smile lifted his lips. His gaze fell on the grass, searching for nothing as his mind seemed to work on overdrive. "I think—If I remember correctly, it's the entrance to the game itself, the AI."

Scarlet and I exchanged looks. Neither of us was tech-savvy.

"Explain it to me like I'm a four-year-old," I said. I winced. Wendy was four. It felt too long since I'd last seen her. This whole grandparent's trip didn't sit well with me, though Kai's parents were the warmest, most loving people I'd ever met. I hated being away from my daughter for so long.

"Artificial intelligence," Carlo said confidently.

"Right."

He scratched at his nose. "Well, it is the access port to the program. It's where someone could reach the code that controls the game." With each word, his eyes widened as if he was surprised to have that knowledge.

"The weird thing is that it's not some medieval knight or king, it's Alice. I'd have thought that the changes from the original game's design would have reached the control panel whatchamacallit." I waved my hand like a wand. Maybe it'd magically help me understand technology and gaming acronyms.

Carlo sucked in a breath, and his eyeballs nearly popped out of his skull. "It's because I created it. I remember now!" He raised his arms in a stiff but excited gesture. "But someone must have overridden the system. Something changed it."

"The new gaming company?"

He pinched his face. "New gaming company... They changed everything."

"Yes, we knew that."

"These aren't updates." His gaze flicked from the grass at our feet to me. "It's a corruption to the original code."

Scar and I both arched an eyebrow in synchronized confusion. I barely understood what Carlo's epiphany meant, but I recognized one very important word: corruption.

Chapter 12

Clouds on the Horizon

T-Minus twenty-something hours until the game would cycle into a major corruption overhaul and erase Carlo's consciousness forever. He'd be trapped in a purgatory of nothingness. Whether he'd remain aware or not, we didn't know. Either way, the diagnosis wasn't good.

I'd tried willing the portal to expand the way I simply thought of the hood and it'd materialize over my shoulders. Next, I repeated the process Scarlet said *call to the story aura, feel it in your fingers.* I traced a door shape in the barrier where I felt the line of thick pressure, but nothing glow or appeared as it once did under Scar's magical command.

Finally, I pushed inside the space but didn't make it through before my throat squeezed and black specks dotted my vision.

I wedged out of the pressure chamber, right through the open white iron gate, and dropped to the field's floor, gasping for breath. Grass tickled and scratched at my legs through the thin fabric of the medieval-style skirts. Nothing worked.

Absent-mindedly, my hand found my stomach, and I rested my open palm on the flat surface. The impossible feat of portal creation reminded me of something else, something I couldn't control no matter how hard I tried and how much I planned, organized sexy time, and tracked my ovulation.

"Without the login lobby, we can't get his address." I sighed, trying to work the details out aloud. But my riffing partner wasn't here. Kai would often brainstorm with me until randomly spouted ideas would spark an epiphany. Scarlet had served as a decent substitute in the past, but nobody quite *got* me like my husband.

"I'm okay with it," Carlo said. His voice came out splintered and stiff, but it still worked, for now.

I looked up at him, expecting to see sadness twisting his face. Instead, the wooden boy wasn't a boy. He was a young man, confident and clear-headed.

"This condition is affecting my body, and the game is affecting my mind. Even if I get out of here before the content erases, I won't be able to move or breathe. I came here as an escape and I know it was my choice to stay as long as I did. Games are my happy place, but it's changing now." He glanced at his frozen fingers that jutted like branches from his hands and almost smiled. In fact, he sounded bright and positive. Perhaps death would be a release from the stress and pain he'd suffered. "I'm okay with letting go."

The honesty in his voice struck through my chest and caused my heart to skip a beat. This young man was a thousand times braver than I'd ever been. Here I was, pitying myself for a few unhappy endings to stories, and how the hood had messed with my life while possibly making me unable to get pregnant. Those things sucked, but they paled compared to Carlo's suffering.

Even if we made it to the login lobby, snagged Carlo's real-world location through the IP address, and got the headset off of him in time, we'd still need to figure out how to stop the reverse Pinocchio process. A real man was turning into a wooden doll right before our eyes. What caused this story to play out backward?

A faint breeze blew through what was left of the field. It tossed the long strands of hair into my face, something of which I wasn't used to since my real-world hair was cropped to just below my chin.

I stood and tried entering the clearing again, only to suffocate a second time. I grabbed Scarlet and Carlo and tried pulling them inside, but they couldn't move past the barrier. This was a connection between stories, just like when Scar had created portals—she'd shift from story aura location to another story aura location.

"Wait, this is the mad hatter's tea party," I said. "I just need another piece of the story." The Alice in Wonderland pieces didn't have the story aura, but neither did Carlo, not inside the game anyway. I pressed against the barrier, feeling the weight of pressure against my palm. It was worth a try—a last-ditch effort.

I squeezed my eyes shut and pictured the *drink me* potion I'd spied in the tavern. The two bits of Alice's story came together in my mind, she'd grown oversized, and shrunk small, she'd fallen down a rabbit hole, spoken with the Cheshire cat, and drank tea with the mad hatter in a place just like this. What else happened in that scene? I wracked my brain, imagining myself rifling through filing drawers filled with colorful, sticky notes.

Finally, the illustrations from Wendy's Wonderland book filled my memory. The Mad Hatter leaned over the table, demanding attention while Alice curiously peered at an object in the March Hare's paw. *A pocket watch*.

My eyes shot open. "Pull up the game's clock."

Scar and Carlo exchanged glances.

"Hurry!"

The clock appeared in the sky above us, a stark reminder that this was a virtual reality—clocks didn't materialize from nothing. But the glitching game was as arbitrary and odd as Wonderland itself.

I stood and pushed past the barrier. The clock's timer froze, fixing time in one place, just as I'd suspected. It matched the Mad Hatter's perpetual tea-time, confirmation that Alice's understanding of the world controlled the game. I held my breath and traced the shape of a door on the barrier from inside the tea party as I visualized the potion that changed Alice's size. Connecting the two would have to work.

For a moment,—or not a moment since time froze—nothing happened.

A crack deafened me, like the sound of lightning striking the Earth.

The fabric of the world ripped and tore in front of me. Where I once saw a field and a ledge of darkness beyond, was now blocked by a tall, wooden door with no knob. I pushed through the barrier. When I stepped back into the field and turned to face the clearing, I could no longer see the table with delicate teacups and frosted small cakes. Instead, round tables, a long bar, and a bustle of players and NPCs welcomed me with a flood of relief.

Scarlet squealed in the silliest barbarian voice. The three of us stepped through the portal and into Fortress Clash's tavern. The portal swirled with the glow of the story magic. I'd created that. Pride swelled in my chest and I knew how Carlo must have felt when he'd remembered he built this game—the original version of it, anyway.

The sight of the Mad Hatter's tea party was the last thing I saw before the portal dissipated. Except one distinction burned in my memory. My jaw dropped as the portal closed, but not before I saw the shape of a dark figure sitting at the end of the table. The cartoonish hat on his head clashed with the muddy, cracked leather jacket.

Was it the Mad Hatter or Johnson?

Scarlet clutched my arm and jumped up and down, rattling me from the moment.

"You did it! You created a portal!"

We'd made it to the fortress, and I nearly laughed to release the stress and tension that had built inside of me. Scar beamed and slapped me on the back in what she meant as friendly, but she'd forgotten her character's strength. The barbarian's hand knocked the wind out of me and I stumbled forward, crashing into another player.

Carlo didn't pay attention to our antics. He'd already disappeared through the door as he walked in awkward angles with jerking movements. We hurried to follow him, exiting the tavern just in time to see him disappear into a small stone building beside the armory.

The little unmarked place was where I remembered entering the game—the login lobby. The door slammed shut as Carlo re-emerged into the cobblestone street only seconds later.

He opened his mouth to speak, but his jaw cracked. "499 Duck

Creek Road, apartment four seventy-nine in San Francisco, California."

We met him halfway across the cobblestone so he wouldn't have to force his joints to bend and crack. I refused to flinch when I reached for his hand, though the wood jabbed the soft flesh of my palm with dozens of tiny splinters.

Carlo tried to open his mouth again, but it was locked and sealed in a straight line like that of a lifeless doll. His dark eyes glistened, and I knew what his tears meant. *Thank you.*

I blinked away the welling emotion in my eyes and squeezed his hands. "See you on the other side."

Chapter 13

The Snowball Effect

Sweat collected under the headset, which left my scalp moist and oily. The headset slipped from my fingers and crashed against the coffee table. My legs buckled beneath me as I collapsed on the cushion of the side chair.

I'd ignored the red tint of the world inside Fortress Clash until we got what we came for. Armed with Carlo's address, I gave myself sixty seconds to breathe before I struggled to my feet again. Exhaustion dragged at my limbs as the constant ache of my throbbing leg and bruised rib sucked my energy dry.

Kai stopped beside the chair on his way to the door and look down at me. While it was a relief to see my husband's actual face and the familiarity of his lean, muscular body, I didn't enjoy the expression that twisted his face. His frown was a waving flag, a reminder that we'd left at a fight. He'd seen through me, reached into my chest, and yanked my heartstrings. He'd tried to pull out of me what I wasn't ready to release, and I didn't have the strength to deal with our tension right now.

I looked away, letting my gaze fall on the window and the sliding glass door that led to our balcony.

"I can't convince you to stay here and rest, can I?" His voice wasn't unkind, but the hint of worry told me he didn't trust me to take care of myself.

I stood and pushed past him without meeting his gaze. "No."

Kai sighed and threw up his hands in frustration. "Scarlet, will you talk some sense into your friend?"

Scar merely blinked.

"My maps app says the drive to Carlo's apartment is almost an hour, including traffic. We need to leave." I said as I slipped my feet into sandals by the door. "Who is coming with me?"

Hair flopped into my husband's face as he shook his head. I wanted to grab him and shake him and spill my confessions to him. *Everything is my fault, I know that. I know you're mad at me. I'm sorry.*

Scarlet crouched and picked up Kai's headset. She brushed her long, smooth curls to one side and balanced the VR equipment like a hat.

"You two go," she said. "I'm going to keep Carlo company while he waits. It's been a long time since I've seen him and it'll be nice to catch up. Especially if he doesn't… you know." I did know, but I wished she hadn't suggested it. The headset fit snugly over her thick hair, and a song from Kai's login lobby was distantly audible.

My husband followed me in silence as we descended the stairs and jumped into the car. Cars lined the streets at rush hour and my ever-patient Kai honked and yelled at other drivers. The celebration of my portal creation was short-lived since coming back to the real world. I couldn't will Kai to calm down or use the story aura to fix our fight.

A streetlight flicked from red to green, and our car jolted forward. I grunted as pain shot up through my ribcage when he slammed the brakes again. The whiplash doubled the ache in my chest.

"I didn't mean to do that," he said. "I didn't want to rear-end the car in front of me—"

"I know."

A throng of pedestrians swarmed the crosswalk in front of us at the next stoplight. Cars beeped and sirens blared from all directions. The city never quieted, so neither did I.

I snuck a glance at my husband. It was clear by the bulge in his jaw that he was grinding his teeth again. His hair looked twisted and mashed from wearing the headset, but he looked as handsome as ever, except for the emptiness in his eyes. He watched the roadblocks and cars around us, but didn't *look* at anything too closely.

I wanted to reach for the hand that rested on his thigh while the other steered the car, but like with the invisible barrier, I couldn't breathe. I'd never taken the time to stop and think about how the Keeper duties affected Kai. He'd been so supportive and ready to help, even when I wanted to throw in the hood and give up.

"We're here," he said as we pulled into a tight parking lot behind a tall building. The climb to the apartment complex's fourth floor left me winded. If I had a health bar in the real world, it would have surely dropped a few percent from the stress of pushing forward when my body craved rest.

Kai banged on the door of apartment four seventy-nine. "Carlo! We're coming in, buddy!"

He waved for me to step back and launched his shoulder into the door. Kai no longer carried the strength of a barbarian with him, and it didn't budge. When he tried again, a familiar sound of splintering wood came from the other side but the door remained intact. He backed up, lifted his leg, and took the door Scarlet-style with the bottom of his foot against the center.

The door cracked from the frame and swung open. Like a portal, it showed a whole new scene on the other side. A weak, mostly wooden guy lay limp on a mattress in a studio apartment so small the kitchen sink nearly reached the bathroom door.

"Carlo!" I rushed into the room and leaned against the bed, suddenly dizzy and lightheaded from the flurry of movement. His skin matched how it had looked in the game, rough and like lumber.

Kai went around the other side of the mattress, squeezing between a sliding closet door and the bed. He leaned over Carlo and yanked at the headset.

"I hope this works."

The headset slipped from Kai's fingers and banged against the wall as it fell off the bed. We both hovered over Carlo and stared, waiting for him to sit up or open his eyes—anything. Could he move with wooden limbs? I gnawed at the inside of my cheek until my mouth hurt.

"He's not waking up," Kai broke the heavy silence.

"I know," I shouted, my voice coming out louder and more intensely than I expected. What else could we do? I started pacing the length of the bed to jog my mind.

"I'm calling an ambulance."

"I can figure something out—"

"Mari." Kai edged around the bed and grabbed my wrist. It forced me to stop pacing and face him. "This isn't about you. You can't fix him without help." He held up the phone. "I'm dialing."

I let my muscles melt and the sense of urgency slipped away from me. There was nothing left I could do for Carlo. The echo of the line trilling came from Kai's cell phone and his voice muted as he gave the first responder Carlo's address.

"What's your emergency?" The woman on the other line asked.

Everything around me dulled.

You can't fix him without help. This isn't about you.

I scrubbed my hand over my face, wiping away the greasy strands of hair that stuck to my temples. In the blur of Kai's voice, Carlo's lifeless body, and my spinning head, I found a seat. I dropped my body into a creaky chair at a tiny kitchen table.

This isn't about you.

Kai's words repeated in my head until tears filled my eyes and spilled down my cheeks. They came fast now, in an uncontrollable flood with gasps of breath and my fists curling until my knuckles turned white. I dropped my face against the heel of my palms and cried until my head rivaled the ache in my rib and leg.

At one point, I registered the first responders crowding into the cramped apartment. They carried Carlo out on a stretcher and exchanged information with Kai. My husband finally materialized in front of me on one knee as he had years ago when he'd proposed.

He took my hand in his and helped me to my feet. I shook my head when he asked if I'd let him take me to the hospital.

"You're worried about me," I stated. I didn't need to ask what I already knew.

"Mari—"

"But you're right, this isn't about me."

"What if we go just to check on Carlo?" My husband changed the subject and with that, I perked up. Maybe he *did* know I wasn't ready to have this conversation. I allowed him to help me into the elevator, and the car, and into the hospital's double doors that sensed our motion and slid open. The drive from Carlo's apartment to the hospital took twice as long as it should have. Thursday rush-hour traffic had shifted into the early start of holiday weekend crowds. The three-day vacation over Labor Day weekend attracted throngs of tourists to the pier. Visitors enjoyed the bay beaches, high-end shopping, and our city's famous clam chowder.

I leaned on Kai's strength as we stepped inside the hospital.

Years ago, I'd run into Scarlet here when she was still the Keeper. It was the same hospital I'd given birth to Wendy and started sensing Red Riding Hood's story aura as growling, howling, and fangs on my OBGYN. I'd avoided the hospital as much as possible since a piece of an investigation here had led to my arrest.

I shoved the flood of memories to the back of my mind with the disorganized file cabinet and mess of imagined sticky notes. By the time we reached the hospital, they had already admitted Carlo from urgent care and moved him upstairs into a room.

Intense cleaning chemicals stung my nose as we made our way down the bright hallway among bustling nurses and doctors. Exhausted loved ones of patients held quiet conversations in hushed tones. We rounded a corner on the second floor and found the room with the number the nurse had given us.

Carlo lay with his limbs in odd positions, all either straight or in perfect right angles, as though he'd been carved. I clung to the hope that the backward story meant it didn't end here. This was the beginning, not the end of Pinocchio, which meant I still had time to twist it. Right?

A woman with a slight frame sat beside his bed with her head buried in her hands. She looked up when we stepped inside.

With a faint nod, she greeted us. Jet black hair framed her face, cropped to the chin with straight bangs over her eyebrows. I wouldn't have pegged the woman to be much older than me. She'd clearly aged with grace. It was the pain in her eyes that yanked at my heart and told me she was Carlo's mother.

"Are you both friends of his?" she asked in a delicate, shaking voice.

"Yes." Kai nodded.

The woman brushed the wetness of tears from below her eyes and sniffled. "He's my son." Tears welled in her dark eyes again, and she turned her head away from us. "I haven't seen him for two years."

Hundreds of people had cried in front of me during interviews before. Witnesses, the victim's loved ones, and even suspects, often had emotional breakdowns when I spoke with them about a murder investigation. Handling emotion wasn't new to me, though I was often a professional expected to gather information. The barrier of professionalism never stopped me from comforting someone in pain, but I rarely crossed the line to physical touch.

This was different.

Mother to mother, I knew she needed the support of a warm embrace. I didn't care if I'd never met her before. I closed the distance from the end of the bed to Carlo's mother and took her into my arms. She accepted, leaning into me while emotion shook her body.

Nothing about the situation was okay, but the rawness of the moment and the connection between two struggling mothers grounded me.

I felt tangible with her weight pressed against me and it gave me the escape from portals, and magic, and fictional worlds that even Fortress Clash's virtual reality couldn't.

I felt alive, and like myself for the first time in a long time.

Carlo's mother sobbed and soiled my shirt. I held her and let her drop the heaviness of her grief in my arms despite the exhaustion that would have ticked my health bar down another percent if this were a game.

But it wasn't. And her pain, though intangible, existed as clearly as the beeping, the chemical smells, and the solid objects surrounding us.

This was real.

Chapter 14

To Make Matters Worse

I'd always been told I had a kind face, the type that caused people to want to open up to me. It helped in my career. But today, I didn't dig for information. Carlo's mother offered it up freely.

"When his condition got worse, he cut everyone off." She cried. I tightened my arms to give the feeling of a weighted blanket around her emotionally exhausted muscles.

Though I didn't intend for the hug to inspire her to speak, she shared her struggles. A mother always recognizes another mother's pain, and it felt good to let this woman relieve the weight of separation.

But the moment wasn't about making me feel good. *Just like stories.* My mind wandered to the hood and my Keeper duties. I'd been obsessed with changing fairy tales and classic plots into cheerful stories to feel like a hero. But helping the innocent people who became storybook characters wasn't a quest in a game meant to make me feel as though I'd accomplished something.

Carlo's mother kept talking. "Doctors didn't know if it was contagious or dangerous, so he put distance between us and all his friends. He even changed his address when I refused to stop visiting him."

It seemed we hadn't been the only people searching for Carlo all this time. No wonder we couldn't track him—he hadn't wanted to be found.

When she gathered her breath and straightened, I let go. The rhythmic beep of the machine attached to Carlo's pulse filled the silence. Footsteps echoed from the busy hallway, then grew louder as a nurse stopped in to check the bag of fluids hanging over Carlo's bed. She nodded and smiled at us as she exited and left us in the room's privacy again.

"I'm Sora," his mother said, extending her hand. "It is nice to hear Carlo had some friends left. He's had a rough life after his father left us in Japan to move back to Italy. We came to San Francisco so Carlo could apply to the tech companies here. Then he developed this…" Sora brushed her fingers over the timber that stiffened the back of his hand. "Condition."

"I'm sorry to hear that," I said lamely. I had many phrases to comfort people with, but this woman's situation was different. What could I say to a mother whose son had disappeared for two years? I couldn't even accept that Wendy was ready for preschool.

"Carlo was a good boy," she said as she patted his arm. "His love for games and computers never alienated me. He even named his new creation after my favorite story character."

"Was it Alice in Wonderland, by any chance?" I asked.

Sora nodded and slipped her hand into Carlo's unmoving fingers. The gesture seemed to pull the two family members into a personal bubble as his mother fixed her gaze on him. Sadness tugged at the corners of her mouth and the silence extended.

"I used to read it to him every night after his father left us. Something about how Alice could change the world fascinated him." After several minutes, Sora looked lost in her own world, as though she'd forgotten we were in the room with her.

It wasn't unlike when I'd repeatedly hugged Wendy on her first day at Everly Woods. I ignored the teacher, the other kids, and that I should drop her off and allow her to learn and grow. While I'd needed to give my daughter some space, Sora was just returning to Carlo's presence.

Something tickled the back of my arm and I turned to see Kai tilt his head toward the door. I nodded, opened my mouth to say goodbye, and thought better of it. Sora needed time to grieve, not an interruption from two strangers.

I let Kai press his hand to the small of my back and guide me out of the room and into the elevator. The doors dinged and slid shut before the box jolted. We descended, dropping to the first floor, but the motion left my stomach swimming. Sickness rose in my throat and stung the back of my tongue with the bitter taste of bile. When we landed on the first floor, the doors chimed again and rolled to reveal the hospital lobby. The rush of chemical smells sent my stomach flip-flopping again, but the contents stayed in place instead of pushing up my throat again.

"You were right," I said with a sigh. We exited the elevator before the doors could trap us inside. "I don't know what has gotten into me lately."

Kai weaved his fingers through mine and squeezed. "You're under a lot of stress."

"We both are." I stopped and turned to him in the middle of the lobby. A nurse pushed a man in a wheelchair past us while the front desk greeted a worried-looking woman who carried a small child. Another woman, swollen with pregnancy, waddled into the elevator as she cupped her heavy belly. The fatigue on her face was clear.

Everyone had their own unique struggles. While mine involved magical hoods and fictional creatures, it wasn't that different. We each struggled with loss, change, exhaustion, and fear. I wasn't special, but I was the Keeper of Stories, and with the hood came great responsibility.

Okay, Scarlet has gotten into my head with the movie quotes. I related to Spiderman, but I almost preferred that a serial-killing wolf had bitten me rather than a spider. I hated spiders.

"I'm sorry," I said, as I returned Kai's squeeze. Instead of a smile accepting my apology, Kai frowned.

"For what?" The pinch of his brow told me he had no clue what I was getting at.

"I forget you're dealing with our infertility, too." I swallowed. Even if I wasn't ready to face the truth yet, I'd spent too long focused on myself. "And I didn't even think about how the Keeper work is stressful for you. I've been feeling like a failure and it just consumes me."

"It's okay, Mar."

I shook my head. "It's not." Emotion bubbled in my chest, pushing up my throat in a painful lump. The hospital smell, the weight of my realization, and the lingering motion sickness from the elevator combined for the perfect storm. I slapped my hand over my mouth. Kai asked if I was okay, but I only managed a one-word response.

"Bathroom."

The blue circle sign caught my eye across the lobby and I nearly dove through the swinging door. After I stumbled into the private bathroom, I bent over the toilet and heaved. Puke tinted the clear water yellow. I grimaced and wiped my mouth, grateful that this wasn't a bathroom with multiple stalls where others could hear my sickness. My stomach lurched again, but nothing came out. The Carlo quest in Fortress Clash had successfully distracted me from my messy life, but it'd also made me forget to eat.

I pulled my phone from my pocket and shot Kai a text.

Will you grab me a pregnancy test from the pharmacy?

Three dots appeared until a thumbs-up emoji popped into the text thread. Ten minutes later, he knocked at the door and I let him in. Kai produced a purple box and a bag of trail mix from the vending machine.

"I thought getting some food in your stomach might help." He leaned against the baby changing table that was attached and folded into the tiled wall while I crouched over the pregnancy test.

If I could click a button to produce a floating clock in the space above us, I would. Instead, I set the timer on my phone to check the pee stick in five minutes as per the instructions on the box. The silence between us felt like a false sense of hope, so I forced myself to face the rest of our interrupted conversation.

"I'm sorry I've been running away."

"That's enough apologies for one day," Kai said, as he brushed strands of hair from my face and tucked them behind my ear. Despite the surroundings of the stark hospital bathroom that stunk of puke and cleaning chemicals, I cupped my husband's face and pulled him into mine. The toilet-adjacent kiss was the opposite of the romance portrayed in a movie, but it had more sentimentality than Hallmark's entire channel. I never liked those sappy sweet stories anyway—life never ended in a happily ever after with a bow as perfect as holiday wrapping. Maybe I needed to stop chasing the impossibility of stories without pain. Was it my job to rid the fairy tales of all pain and suffering? Or merely to help innocent people as best as I could?

Kai wrapped his arms around my lower back and our lips pressed together with intention and vulnerability.

Though our kiss lasted only seconds, it was the second moment that day to remind me I was alive—this was real. Real life was full of passion and love and pain. Sora's story proved that an escape into distraction would never completely free us from this, though I couldn't fault Carlo for trying to protect her and using the game to relieve harsh truths.

I closed the top of the toilet and took a seat, letting my body's muscles relax while my emotional muscles flexed. The minutes passed so slowly that I almost thought we were back in the Mad Hatter's tea party, where time froze. I balanced the pregnancy test on the edge of the sink and raked my fingers through my greasy hair.

My phone buzzed, but it wasn't the timer. The clock still ticked, slowly but relentlessly. I tapped the rectangle at the top of the screen to bring up the text thread between Scarlet, Kai, and me.

Scarlet: What happened? It's been hours since I've heard from you guys and Carlo's gone now.

I tapped away at the digital keyboard to ensure Scar we'd gotten to Carlo in time. Their friendship wasn't one I'd thought about much over the past several years. Scar mentioned Carlo, but I'd assumed it was related to my search for him and her obsession with the story cycle. Another reminder that I'd become so self-absorbed I'd blinded myself to the reality right in front of me. My best friend cared about Carlo and likely didn't want to join us on the trip to his house, where she'd be forced to acknowledge his sickness.

I couldn't blame her for pretending it wasn't as bad as we'd thought. It was worse.

The dots appeared under my response and Scarlet's message popped up before I could swipe back to the timer app.

Scarlet: Is Carlo okay? He kept rambling on about someone named Alice. Do you know what that means? Alice this and Alice that. He said Alice knows him better than anyone else.

I frowned and furrowed my brow. My phone vibrated, and the timer covered the screen.

Alice? As in the game he created? One thing at a time, Mari. After a cleansing breath, I glanced at Kai, who nodded. He was ready for the answer.

I pinched the pee stick and chewed my lip. The tiny test window displayed one lone pink line—negative.

I stood and folded my arms, bringing the test to my chest and leaning into my husband. Tears didn't come, but I stayed in his hold until the motion-sensing light above us flicked off. It left us in total darkness. The warmth of Kai's body kept me upright.

In the silence, my mind repeated the same thought I'd questioned earlier. Except now, it'd changed to a statement—I was sure of it now.

It *wasn't* the Keeper's job to wipe out pain and suffering from the fairy tales. Stories had conflict because they represented the one thing I'd been running from for so long.

"It's going to be okay," Kai said.

"I know."

Chapter 15

Against the Clock

With the game returned to Fortress Clash, Carlo under the care of doctors, and our last day with Wendy at her grandparent's house, we slept in. It wasn't intentional, but my body demanded rest after the emotional rollercoaster of the past few days.

The alarm that woke me didn't budge Kai from his soft snoring. Scar groaned loud enough that I could hear her from the bedroom. Kai's phone trilled obnoxiously again until I finally threw the comforter off my legs and padded around to the nightstand on his side of the bed.

Pier 39 Fertility Cen...

The phone's narrow screen cut off the rest of the clinic's title. I hesitated with my shaking thumb over the answer button. We'd already lost the morning hours, and I needed to dive back into the game to track down Johnson. Answers about the story cycle were so close I could almost taste them—or that was the bitterness of morning breath on my tongue.

At the last second, I slid my thumb across the button and brought the phone to my ear.

"Mr. Rowan, we have an opening today for an appointment and you were next on our waitlist."

"What?" I coughed to clear the squeakiness from my throat. "What happens at the first appointment?"

The man's bright voice reminded me of Wendy's preschool teacher. They'd make a perfect pair. "We'll go over your medical histories and the timing and frequency of intercourse. We'll also need to discuss fertility tests for each of you."

I nodded, then realized he couldn't see me and the phone wasn't a headset. "Okay, when is the appointment?"

"In an hour."

My jaw dropped, and I glanced down at my giant oversized T-shirt and pink pajama pants. I could dress quickly and play the part of the polite patient. That wasn't the problem. Taking the opportunity was the logical thing to do, though the slight shake in my hands and sickness in my stomach didn't agree.

I'd planned to spend the day back inside the game, practicing with portals to track Johnson. A last-minute change of plans didn't sit well with my usual order of business.

Kai sighed in his sleep and rolled in the other direction. I wasn't the only one wanting answers—answers we could get from Pier 39 Fertility Clinic.

Before I could chicken out and run away again, I spoke. "We'll take it."

Scar agreed to hold down the fort while we left, which meant she'd mill around in Fortress Clash and dig for clues about where Johnson could hide before the game finished updating. She swooped me into an awkward hug—she was slowly getting better at normal human interaction but didn't quite master it yet.

"I bet you'll get pregnant with like eight babies," she said.

"Uh, thanks?"

The smell of Eggo waffles drifted from the kitchen. The toaster launched our to-go breakfast up and Kai caught them mid-air. He slapped them on paper plates. When he rounded the counter and offered me one, I shook my head.

"What if it's the hood?" I tugged at the strings that dangled over my collarbone. Scar's gaze dropped to my fidgeting fingers and her expression turned thoughtful.

"How would that work?" Kai asked, as he took a bite of the plain waffle and munched.

"The hood controls the wearer's destiny," Scar said. "It's possible, since your destiny is to be the Keeper of Stories."

"Not if I give it to someone else." I nodded toward the discarded headsets piled against the coffee table. "What if Johnson is a Keeper too?"

The fear that twisted Scar's face left my stomach unsettled. I swallowed saliva to get a head start on keeping the contents of my stomach pressed down where they belonged. She tucked her curls behind her ears and opened her mouth.

Before she could argue, I turned. "We'll be late if we don't leave now."

Kai nodded, stuffed the last of the Eggos into his mouth, then launched the empty paper plate into the kitchen like a frisbee.

The short drive to the fertility center didn't give me enough time to prepare mentally, but warm colors and comfortable couches welcomed us into the office. The receptionist's cheerful smile solidified the positivity of the place. It wasn't until we were closed in a small private room that I noticed the pamphlets with needles and bloodwork. I grimaced and folded the glossy pages back into a neat little rectangle, then slipped it into the clear holding case attached to the wall.

Artwork on the walls and soft chairs only partially covered the clinical atmosphere. It didn't match the hospital, but I couldn't help thinking about Carlo with the faint scent of cleaning chemicals stinging my nose.

Who was I kidding? I hadn't gotten my mind off of the story cycle since I accepted the hood. It'd only gotten worse now that I realized I wasn't doing any good.

The doctor entered with a smile that rivaled her receptionist's and extended a warm hand to greet us. The conversation started off with a bang and the busy specialist didn't waste a second of our appointment. After a blunt discussion of our medical histories, and an uncomfortable introduction to all the tests we'd have to undergo, the doctor folded her hands in her lap and paused.

The moment of silence gave us the opportunity to decide if we wanted to pursue testing. We exchanged glances and Kai reached for my lap, taking my hand in his. It was his answer—he wanted me to decide. My stomach let out an angry groan in protest at not eating breakfast. The doctor tucked her dark hair behind her ears and pretended not to notice the riot in my belly. It was the least she could do after bombarding us with information about necessary testing and the emotional turmoil that it often caused.

I opened my mouth, hoping the answer would come out without me having to decide. I couldn't muster my voice, but the doctor filled the silence for me.

"I'm sensing you're the organizer out of the two of you." She held my gaze. "Stress alone rarely causes fertility issues, but its effects can. Are you eating a balanced diet and sleeping regularly?"

The doctor saw right through my pathetic shrug. She clucked her tongue, but the soft expression on her face wasn't condescending. Instead, she curled her lips into an apologetic smile and nodded.

"If you're not comfortable starting fertility treatments just yet, try to cut back on the planning."

Kai side-eyed me, and I knew he was thinking the same thing. The over-stuffed planner sitting on our kitchen table, the ovulation tracking app on my phone, and the mountains of sticky notes around our house were tangible proof of my scheduling obsession. Though it had gotten better with time, our attempts to conceive sent me back into an organized frenzy.

The doctor patted my knee and stood. "Some couples have found that simply relaxing and taking the pressure off of conception helps them get pregnant. Since you're not ready for testing, my advice is to let go a little. When I'm overwhelmed, I like to do a little thought exercise and some of my patients have found comfort in it. You write all your fears, hopes, dreams, and thoughts about pregnancy and then store them away. It tricks your brain into relieving the overthinking but keeps you feeling like you didn't give up since you save the information in a journal or notebook."

"Or a computer," I muttered. Speaking of thoughts, my mind tumbled to pieces of the puzzle. Despite the doctor's suggestions, I organized twice as hard.

"Sure, sure, wherever you prefer to write things down." The doctor didn't pick up on my brainstorming, but Kai did.

He tilted his head and furrowed his brows. "What're you thinking?"

"We need to go." I leaped up. The doctor raised her eyebrows and looked between us, but I didn't bother to explain. I shoved through the door, leaving the doctor and the fertility center in the dust.

Exhaustion or not, I didn't slow down. Kai followed at my heels and asked for clarification as we dropped into the front seats of our car. The car ride gave me time to gather my thoughts. The unspoken agreement between us eased me. Kai and I were a team again, as clear by his trust in me to make the fertility treatment decision.

For now, I allowed myself to focus on the investigation. I bounced ideas off of Kai while he drove. It took a lot of Googling on my phone, but we pieced together a basic understanding of artificial intelligence and computer code. Corruption to the game translated from a file that was overtaking the original code and changing it. The access port, ALICE, was the location of the change, which meant it contained something I'd need to remove or fix.

"Maybe a CD?" I asked.

Kai laughed. "I'm sorry, but what century are you living in?"

I frowned. Centuries were a sore subject. "I was a nineties kid, so what? At least I didn't call it a floppy disk."

The car revved as Kai stepped on the gas to make it through a yellow stoplight before it shifted to red. "No, like a corrupted code, or flash drive, or a computer virus."

Gratitude filled me at Kai's slightly better understanding of technology and games. A history nerd didn't delve into the virtual world often, but he'd had his moments with video games to relieve stress after a long day dealing with obnoxious teenagers who refused to learn about world governments.

I jabbed the handle to the glove box until it fell open and revealed a block of to-go Post-It notes.

T-Minus 2 hours until the updates—or corruption changes—finished.

In green, I scribbled the pieces I knew about Johnson. *He can create portals. Take on the look of Carlo. He's the only one who can enter the restricted area in the game. Does that mean he's the anonymous company threatening to takeover?*

With orange, I reminded myself of Pinocchio's story. *Log carved into a puppet. Puppet misbehaves and dies, but a blue fairy eventually saves him and grants him life as a real boy.*

I peeled off a piece of red from the rainbow of colors and added more notes. *Carlo = Pinocchio but backward. Alice knows him better than anyone else, but Alice is the name of the system he created. Could he have stored his memories in the game?*

Next on the block of colors was blue. I stared at the blank piece of paper and gnawed at the inside of my cheek. The jerky movements of Kai maneuvering the car in Friday traffic bothered my stomach, but I ignored it, too engrossed in the clues.

"This is a stretch but—" I pressed the sticky end of the blue note against the dashboard above the glove box. "That's the color of Alice's dress, right?"

Kai pulled the car into the covered spot at our apartment, shifted the gear into park, and looked at the blank Post-It with his brow pinched. "I guess?"

"And a blue fairy saves Pinocchio, but in all the fictional things I've ever seen come alive, I've yet to meet this fairy. Where is the rest of Pinocchio's story?"

Kai scratched the back of his neck before dropping his hands on his lap. "I couldn't tell you. Oh—" he shifted to face me. "When you were on Mr. G's account in Fortress Clash, you said you saw the story aura in the game. But you didn't mention it when you made a character of your own."

I gasped. I'd forgotten about the glittering beige trail that had lured me out of the fortress. "You're a genius!" Excitement had me clutching his arm with my fingernails digging into his shirtsleeve. "If Carlo stored himself inside the game, maybe that means everything about Pinocchio's story is attached to Fortress Clash."

"So, when Mr. G is playing the game, he's a story character, but when he logs out—"

"He doesn't have the story aura."

Kai crossed his arms. "So what's the stretch? That all makes sense."

I tapped the blue sticky note. "Does the color of Alice's dress match her to the fairy?"

Without a response, Kai exited the car and headed for the staircase. I slid out of my seat and hurried after him.

"Do you think I'm crazy?"

"Definitely," he said over his shoulder. "But your *crazy* is usually right. So, let's do this." We climbed the staircase and the sense of urgency returned. I took two steps at a time and huffed and puffed until we burst through the front door.

I slipped off my shoes and picked up a headset at Scar's feet. If she heard us come in, she didn't show it. She stood, entranced by the game, with only slight movements clicking the controls. It impressed me she'd gone from not knowing what a TV is called to managing a video game, but it didn't surprise me. After teaching her in the internship at Bay Side Media for a year, I knew Scarlet was a fast learner when she wanted to be. Nothing was impossible with her can-do attitude and relentless determination.

Kai's phone trilled. When he answered, I caught the tone of his voice before he disappeared into the bedroom. The high-pitched, sweet pitch only came out when he spoke with one particular person.

If I dropped the headset and took a few minutes to chat with Wendy over the phone, it'd soak up the last bits of time I had left to help Carlo before the content vanished. My leg bounced without my permission.

"I miss you," Kai's voice drifted from the other room.

When Wendy returned home tomorrow, I'd have all the time in the world with her. The vacation at her grandparents' would have plenty of memories for her to share. Plus, they probably packed her with a ton of sugar and she'd beg me to take her to the park. She didn't need me right now, but Carlo did.

I groaned and tugged the headset on. The special song in my unique login lobby chimed. My character, nearly identical to me, dropped into the game. The resting period of leaving the character in the fortress had restored some of the green on my health bar. If only I'd take time to rest in the real world, I might get pregnant again. I reached for the strings of the hood but remembered my hands each held a controller.

With a click, I opened the door to my lobby and stepped out onto the cobblestone street. Fortress Clash was a ghost town now, abandoned by players who had gotten their fill of loot before the corruption wiped the content—Carlo's content.

I sent my character jogging to the tavern. The fastest route to the Mad Hatter's tea party would be a portal, but that didn't guarantee I'd reach Alice without suffocating first. Carnage covered the streets with NPC bodies strewn over the cobblestone. It sickened me how quickly the players turned violent for a bit of loot. Of course, it was only a game—they didn't know a young man's entire life was attached to it.

Beyond the gates, darkness seeped into the fortress area. I picked up the pace. The changes would likely boot me from the game as soon as they reached me.

After dodging blood stains and limp characters, I picked my way into the tavern. The boisterous, lively drinking atmosphere had been reduced to an empty building. The bar tending NPC repeatedly wiped the counters, stuck in an endless loop before he'd wipe off the map forever. It spared him for now. I slipped behind the counter and opened all the cabinets. Bottles clinked and only felt from an over-packed shelf as I slammed cabinets that had nothing to offer me.

Finally, I found the drink me potion and picked it up. Sure enough, a faint beige glow surrounded out. I took a whiff of the fruity smell and wrinkled my nose. The potion came from *Alice's Adventures in Wonderland*, yet it showed the color of Pinocchio's story aura. I logged the clue away as confirmation that everything Carlo had created here was connected to him and his fairy tale. Classic story? I wasn't sure what to call the wooden boy's adventures.

"Mari?" A voice interrupted my thoughts, and I spun around to see the one person who'd know the answer to that question—wait, not the only one. Johnson was in here somewhere too, and if he knew how to create portals, he knew a lot more than I did.

Bouncing red curls cascaded over Scarlet's bony shoulders. She looked like herself again in the old-world style dress and naturally ruby lips. Like me, she'd designed her character to match what she saw in the mirror. But for Scar, she saw a young girl from four hundred years ago—not the woman she'd grown into today.

"Are you here to give up the hood?" Her gigantic eyes scanned me carefully. Did that mean she'd found Johnson?

Instead of answering her question, I shifted the subject to the immediate problem. "I want to find him," I admitted. "But first I need to talk to Alice."

Scarlet recoiled and frowned. "Alice? The girl Carlo is obsessed with?" She shook her head. "If you're thinking it's the Alice from the fairy tale, you're wrong. I already sealed her fairy tale this century, before you came around."

"She's part of the game," I said. "Not the real character, person, thing, but a game based on her."

The shadow of a massive figure cast over Scarlet. My breath caught in my throat, not knowing what to expect from the game that had turned into The Purge. I couldn't help it, the game had hurt me before. What could a powerful player do to me?

The man stomped into the tavern, and dim lights filled in his features. Though his meaty neck and hulk shoulders didn't resemble Kai, I recognized his character. Breath returned to my lungs.

"Mari's got a nutty idea and it just might work."

I nodded. "Carlo created Alice and since he claimed she knows him so well, I'm thinking he stored his memories inside the game. Since he didn't wake up when we removed the headset, we need to access his consciousness or soul or whatever it is by fixing Alice.

She's the computer program that's been corrupted. I think…" I bounced my fist against the bar top. "I think Alice could be the blue fairy."

"But Pinocchio is playing out backward," she argued.

"True, but either way, he's a wooden puppet who wants to be a real boy. You told me the blue fairy is the only thing that has ever fixed him," I explained.

"This is Carlo though—" she stopped. Scar's character vanished. Even though I knew she couldn't create portals anymore, she'd become a regular San Francisco mortal. It still tripped up my brain. She didn't use magic or story aura to teleport away. She'd simply removed the headset Mr. G left in our living room.

I pulled at mine but couldn't feel anything tangible. Thumping sped in my chest as I waved my arms around. My character looked frantic or desperate to get someone's attention, but I didn't register anything solid in the real world.

"Kai, I'm stuck!" As I said it, I felt the cold plastic of the headset against my palms. With a push, I freed myself from Fortress Clash and scanned the room. Scarlet was gone. A cabinet in the kitchen banged shut, and I whipped my head in that direction.

Scar snatched a bottle of vodka from the top of our refrigerator and dumped half a glass full of the clear liquid. Without hesitation, she knocked the cup back and downed three shots worth of alcohol in one swig.

"Dang," Kai mumbled. He'd removed his headset.

"Stop staring. I'm not a zoo animal," Scarlet snapped. The slap of the glass on the counter convinced me it'd break. When it didn't, Scarlet rested her palms against the tile and let her head hang between her shoulders.

"What's going on?" I asked.

Scar played with a dish towel she'd found on the counter. It twisted and tangled as she turned it over in her hands. "Nothing."

I scoffed. "That's a lie."

Without lifting her head, Scarlet flicked her gaze up at me. Through the overhang over her brow and the bushy, thick mane of hair surrounding her face, she looked like an angry lion, ready to pounce. "If I say it's nothing, then it's nothing."

"Fine." I shrugged. I loved her, but if she didn't want to talk, I didn't have precious moments to waste. "Good. I need to get back to it." I grabbed the headset, but the sound of glass clinking against the counter stopped me from pulling it on.

Scar poured herself another shot and threw her head back for a quick gulp. "How can a game be the blue fairy?"

"How can fictional characters come to life?" I countered with my hands up in mock surrender. "I don't know, Scar. I'm grasping at straws here. Carlo didn't wake up, but he's still turning into Pinocchio. I have to try, don't I?"

A sudden sob escaped her, and she leaned over the counter, dropping her head in her hands. Scarlet's shoulders shuddered. Before I could move, Kai hurried into the kitchen and pulled her into a hug. He shot me a worried look with a slight shrug.

"He's my friend," Scar cried. "Carlo was my friend."

She'd never mentioned it before. Sure, she showed a mild interest in him, but I'd always assumed it was his relation to the Pinocchio classic. Scar always showed an interest in fairy tales and story aura. It was her existence for hundreds of years. It suddenly struck me I didn't know Scarlet as well as I liked to believe.

After she'd stayed with us, I'd chalked her up to a whip-smart but clueless young woman who needed a lot of guidance to make it in the real world. Eventually, we became friends and then I'd hired her as my assisting intern, but we never went in-depth. Scar spoke in TV and movie quotes, threw herself into investigations, and enjoyed babysitting Wendy. But other than those basic details and a few mild dates with guys in the city, Scarlet didn't have dreams or deep feelings about anything beyond classic stories and fairy tales.

Or so I'd thought. Scarlet cared about Carlo, and I'd had no idea. Disappointment in myself dragged my shoulders even lower than exhaustion already had.

Once again, I'd been so wrapped up in my pity-party issues I'd completely missed my best friend's suffering.

Chapter 16

Bell the Cat

Like the father of all who needed comforting, Kai kept Scarlet wrapped in a warm hug until her sobbing slowed. He reminded me of the snowman from Wendy's favorite movie. To him, Scar was another daughter who needed his Olaf-style hugs and jokes to cheer her up.

Kai nodded, a signal that it was okay for me to return to the game. I allowed myself to pull the headset over my eyes. He'd save Scarlet's day while I saved Carlo's. It would all work out. It *must*.

My character materialized in the tavern. Without Kai and Scarlet, the eerie silence tugged at me. The repetitive motion of the broken NPC's cleaning left me with chills. I didn't look forward to seeing Alice again with her dead, unfocusing eyes and dialogue stuck on repeat. Would Johnson be there, too?

I blew out a slow breath and started tracing the shape of a door near Pinocchio's aura that surrounded the bottle with the *drink me* tag. As I pictured the Mad Hatter's tea party with the delicate dishes and decadent cakes, the glow of the portal cut through to the other side. The scene with the table in the clearing filled in with each inch I added to the door. I swallowed the thickness in my throat and stepped through.

Immediately, the unwelcome pressure beat down on my shoulders and chest. I wanted air, but there was none. I tried to ignore the squeeze in my lungs as I pushed toward the table. The sky blue of Alice's dress caught my eye, and I made my way toward her. From a distance, I couldn't decipher what was on the screen in the book. What did I expect to see? Would the virus butcher the picture on the screen? Or did the book have a flash drive in it?

I was in over my head, but that wouldn't stop me from trying. I reached into my pocket for the stopwatch I'd figured out how to access after watching Carlo.

T-Minus fifty-eight minutes until the 'updates' finished and changed everything. After shoving forward, I made it to the access port. Alice greeted me on cue with her creepy, monotonous voice.

I tapped at the keyboard, pressing buttons methodically. After spelling out Carlo, Alice, and Sora, I gathered the courage to smash the Escape button. It only returned the screen on the righthand side back to the base that said ALICE and cleared away all of my typing.

If I could breathe, I'd groan. In the time it took to exit the restricted clearing, take a cleansing breath, and return, I'd lost almost four minutes. Sweat beaded on my forehead and my stomach twisted as I pushed back toward the tea party.

The silhouette of a dark figure hunched over the end of the table. I froze as he rose with his gaze fixed on me.

"Howdy, Mari." Johnson winked, and a smirk curved one side of his lips.

I opened my mouth but remembered I couldn't speak, not without losing too much air. He had the upper hand, all control. When he stood, he bumped into the table and it scooted slightly across the grass. Like Alice, Johnson didn't have a health bar or in-game name floating above his head. Unlike her, he interacted with me clearly. His gaze burned through my skull and the way he moved didn't match the pace and rhythm of the character's gaits.

He was real, existing in the game with his physical body—opposite of Carlo, but not so different from me. I was here, almost, since I could feel my surroundings.

"I thought you'd come here," he spoke as he walked toward me. Butterflies erupted in my stomach at the intensity of his presence. Johnson had changed, grown in confidence and a commanding presence since he'd thrown my mother in a jail cell. "I bet you thought you could fix Alice like you do with those little murder mysteries. I'll admit, when the blue fairy showed up as a computer program, I wanted to punch somebody." He squeezed his fist and made a face that reflected his past anger. "I miss the good ol' days when characters were people, not artificial intelligence. But it wasn't as much work as I thought to learn a few new things and hack in. Definitely worth it to bring you here."

Alice is the blue fairy. I was right. Despite the miniature accomplishment, I frowned.

Johnson smirked. "It's always worth it to please the gods."

I didn't want to know what that meant. This dude was absolutely off his rocker, and I didn't want to stick around to deal with it. But he had control over the blue fairy, which meant I couldn't save Carlo without his cooperation.

Johnson circled me and raked his eyes over my body. I needed air. Time ran thin on my ability to hold my breath.

"You want to help Carlo? Is that correct?"

I said nothing, only offering him a frown.

He took a long breath. Was he mocking my struggle? "I'd like to propose a trade. Alice for the cloak."

The cloak? Did he mean my hood?

When Johnson dropped his hand on my shoulder, I curled my hands into fists, ready to strike him the way I'd learned in self-defense classes. But I didn't have the energy, not without a fresh dose of oxygen.

He grimaced and pulled his hand back. "I can see the cloak, but I can't feel it."

He doesn't realize I'm not in the game. Did that mean he knew something I didn't? Could I physically enter Fortress Clash from my living room?

Maybe, but I'd need the aura. If I could create a portal from story aura to story aura, then I could move into the game because of Pinocchio's consciousness here. But did I want to?

The tightness in my chest threatened to send me to the grassy floor. I glanced over my shoulder at the distance between me and the barrier. Johnson stood in the space between. Instead of crossing him, I dropped to a crouch and traced the shape of a door.

The burn in my lungs crawled up my throat and everything within me squeezed tighter. As an adept swimmer, I'd never feared drowning before. Then came the hood and immortality—until the game skirted those too. If I died here, would Kai and Scarlet witness my body collapse on the other side? Was I breathing at home?

No. The visceral pain in my pseudo-body made that clear. Either the game had tricked my senses into believing the virtual world was reality or my magic as the Keeper placed me in a purgatory between portals. I dragged my finger along the ground, but the magic was slow and steady.

Like the corruption in the game's code, blackness seeped into my vision as my body gasped for oxygen. Panic tempted me to stop creating the portal and claw at my shrinking throat. I grabbed at my neck and rocked back and forth. The memory of Frankenstein's monster choking me came rushing back.

Fight it. Keep going.

I jabbed my finger against the ground and reached for the buzzing sensation of the aura of stories. With the potion pictured in my mind, I called forth the tavern on the other side.

I dropped through, collapsing from the ceiling of the tavern to the wooden planks on the floor. Gulping air wasn't possible with the squeeze in my throat. Oxygen came in small doses as I gasped. The impact of the fall left my head throbbing, but I didn't mind the pain since I could breathe here. Before the portal closed, the echo of Johnson's laugh drifted into the tavern.

"You'll be back!" he shouted.

I whipped out the pocket watch and counted the minutes. Twenty-seven ticks to save Carlo's life. What did the doctors think of Carlo's body? It must have been almost entirely made of wood by now.

After clambering to my feet and pacing the length of the bar, I tried another portal, then closed it. I knew the result of skipping from story aura to story aura as a player in the game. What I needed to know was if I could do the same as a person. I talked to the NPC as if he could say anything more than the repetitive dialogue. He wasn't the only one stuck on repeat.

With a fill of air, I opened a portal and stepped into the Mad Hatter's tea party again. The pressure slowed me down, but I could make a run for it. After this, I swore to stop skipping yoga. Maybe I'd even join Kai on a run or two.

I ignored the figure to my right and focused on Alice. She held the key to returning Carlo to himself and I'd find out what it was. The muscles in my legs flexed and burned as I shoved through the pressure. No matter how hard I tried, I'd never beat Johnson to the access port.

Without effort, he stepped in front of me. "Make the trade, Keeper. The gods will bless you. Then you can choose to be free of all of this or help me save the story cycle."

I swallowed, and it seemed my tongue had doubled in size like an allergic reaction to Johnson's offer. Without my permission, my fingers reached for the strings of the hood's tie.

You can be free of this. The ache in my ribcage returned as my heart slammed against the bones. I could strip from the hood, turn around, and never look back. Fairy tales and story monsters would be nothing more than a distant nightmare after I returned to my family. Evil Queens and Ugly Ducklings would stay within the bounds of Wendy's books and I wouldn't have to think twice about sacrificing my fertility, or my life, to save someone else. Maybe I'd have the time and energy to go after a Pulitzer in my career.

I squeezed my eyes shut. My fingers scrambled for the feel of the velvet strings, the bow that fastened the hood, the anchor that dragged me down into the fictional world. If I removed the hood, could I get pregnant? The thought of my destiny becoming my own again filled my stomach with butterflies' wings beating against the boundaries of my body. I willed the hood to materialize and the full sight of it sent Johnson's eyebrows sky-high.

I tugged at the strings, but as they unraveled, Scar's words flooded my mind. *I have a bad feeling about this.* Of course, she did. Johnson corrupted Carlo's consciousness. The man standing before me basically trapped the soul of Sora's son. Who was I to say my freedom from this life was greater than Carlo's life?

It didn't matter. I couldn't decide now, as my body demanded to breathe. Johnson watched as I created a portal and vanished from the clearing. The tavern refreshed my lungs but did nothing to clear my mind from his offer. When I returned, Johnson hadn't moved. He expected me to do this—to give him the hood.

The grin that stretched his dry skin sent my heart to the pit of my stomach. Maybe the butterflies down there could carry it back up to its place beneath my ribcage. For now, I was a mess, twisted inside and sick at myself. Instead of fixing Alice to save Carlo, I could fix myself without the help of a doctor. The risks of being the Keeper of Stories could endanger my family, and I could make it all go away. I could return to my living room and tell Kai that it was all over. I wouldn't live forever. I wouldn't have to watch Wendy grow old without me.

Johnson stepped closer and reached out his hand. "Give me the cloak. I'll right all the stories you wronged and the gods will smile down on both of us."

I clutched the strings to keep the hood from slipping off my shoulders.

"I know you tried." He edged closer, stepping into my personal bubble. "Your family distracted you. Loved ones always weaken us and keep us from doing what needs to be done."

What did that mean? I'd failed to always form a happy ending for every fairy tale, but I'd done *some* good. Right? Kai wouldn't let me forget that.

Johnson sighed and flexed his outstretched hand. "Come on, Mari." His voice dropped an octave and impatience caused a twitch of his cheek. "If you're having second thoughts about leaving this, you can join me. But you'll have to leave your family behind."

My fingers clenched the strings tighter.

"Give it to me!" Johnson shouted in my face and blinked rapidly.

The demand in his voice told me everything I needed to know. He'd knowingly corrupted Carlo. And for what? I couldn't trust him.

"Mari." With a lunge forward, Johnson reached for my neck. A horrible memory flashed across my mind of Frankenstein's thick hands grabbing my throat with the intent to kill. I leaped back.

No. I shook my head.

A strange look overcame him. Johnson's gaze dropped to the ground and wandered in a familiar expression that I'd had many times myself when putting pieces of a puzzle together.

His head snapped up, and his attention returned to me. To my absolute shock, he moved aside and opened his arms as if to say *after you.* If my jaw could drop to the floor, it would have.

I grimaced and took the opportunity to push my way to Alice. The access port lit up as I mashed the Enter button. My hands shook as I tapped the screen and waited for it to demand a password, or expose a virus—anything to signal where I could fix it.

With a quick return to the tavern, I gathered my breath and stepped back into the Mad Hatter's realm. Each time, I called forth the portal magic faster. At least, the stupid pressure chamber forced me to practice the new skill I'd gained.

Alice spoke her programmed dialogue as I approached her again. I typed all the relevant words but had switched from something related to Carlo to Johnson. Words like 'cloak' and 'hood' didn't work. I tried Johnson's name and anything I could think of that was connected to him, but the screen didn't ask for a password. The jumble of words typed into the screen did nothing, and no interruptions indicated a virus in the system.

My throat squeezed, and I grabbed at the book until my knuckles turned white. *How do I fix you?* Where was the corruption? Frustration built with the burning in my chest. I shook her and opened my mouth to release the anger in a scream.

"Keep trying, Mari," Johnson said with a laugh. "Don't give up." His hot breath tickled the back of my neck, but when I turned, he was gone. Where he'd stood, a portal filled the space. I didn't recognize the scene on the other side of a rural town with a red barn in the distance.

A white farmhouse with a large wrapping porch and two rocking chairs was the closest building.

My body begged for me to dive through the opening and suck in the sweet air, but I couldn't confirm if this new location was between portals.

Instead, I called for my magic as the Keeper and desperately drew another portal that carried me to the tavern once again. I slammed my fist against the bar, but the NPC didn't react. It only hurt my fingers and frustrated me more.

I needed to try something different. With that, I yanked the headset from my face. Chaos greeted me.

Scarlet was curled on the countertop with her arms hugging her knees and a tissue sticking out of her nose. Instead of blood, it stopped the flow of snot from the end of a long sob session. That didn't surprise me so much as the four-year-old darting around the room with a giant rainbow lollipop in her hand.

"Mommy!" Wendy dove off the couch and launched herself into my arms. I huffed as her body collided with my chest. I caught her and returned her sweet hug, but shot Kai a confused look. He raked his fingers through his overgrown hair that flopped into his face as he shrugged.

"Mom and Dad dropped her off a day early. They said she missed you too much. Did you fix the file?"

I shook my head. "Johnson is there. I need to try creating a portal from outside the game to the Mad Hatter's tea party so I can deal with him on his level. Or at least, so I can be there long enough to make a deal with him."

Scarlet's head shot up and unfolded herself. After she hopped off the counter and unplugged the wadded tissue from her nostrils, she chimed in the conversation.

"Don't trade the hood," she begged. "I have such a bad feeling about him. I can't explain it. I—"

"All I'm doing is trying to get to the AI so I can figure out whatever is corrupting it and help Carlo."

Scarlet curled her bottom lip under and chewed the chapped skin.

"How are you going to create a portal from here? You need the story aura."

At that precise moment, a portal opened without my permission. In the wall where Scarlet had ripped the fabric of reality once before when she'd still been the Keeper of Stories, a door opened. Wendy shrieked and scurried to hide behind Kai's legs.

"Did you do that?" I breathed.

Scarlet shook her head. "I can't. Did you?"

The portal showed a glimpse into Fortress Clash, and a figure filled the doorway. Johnson stepped on the threshold between the game and our living room. The scene of the pixilated world on the other side, and me standing her utterly helpless, sent me back to Cygnus Island where I'd first chase him down. He'd tried to trick me into giving him the hood then, and it seemed he wanted the same thing now.

Wendy's whimpers ignited a fire within me. If I rid myself of the hood and the curse of the life that came with it, my daughter wouldn't experience nightmarish men busting through our wall. And maybe, just maybe, she'd get the baby brother she wanted.

Despite the ticking clock and the temptation to untie the hood's strings and throw it at the intruder, one big question distracted me.

If portals could only exist between two areas of story aura, what in our home had become part of an open fairy tale?

Chapter 17

At the 11th Hour

The look of shock on Johnson's face mirrored our expressions. Didn't he intend to come here?

The uneven whiskers on his skin prickled as he frowned. His narrowed gaze fixed on me. "You're supposed to be in the game." The growl in his voice twisted my stomach. I'd fought and killed the serial murderer who'd hunted me when I became Red Riding Hood. I wasn't ready to do it again—except Johnson's eyes weren't hungry for me. The trails of his gaze slipped from my face, down my neck, then landed on my collarbone.

I touched the strings, the only visible part of the hood in the real world. The loose bow that tied them together could be pulled apart with one tug.

Johnson cursed and backed into the portal's world next to the farm-house. The glowing magic dissipated and our wall returned to normal. Good thing I'd never hung out the wedding photograph back on that wall.

"What the hell was that?" My husband's voice squeaked.

"Kai!" I scolded and tilted my head at our miniature, who hid behind his legs. Enormous eyes looked up at us, listening to every word. Curiosity sparkled in her gaze as fear from the intruder melted away.

Kai scrubbed his hand over his face, and he crouched. "I'm sorry, Wednesday."

Wendy brushed the flopped from his face, a gesture she'd seen him do for me many times. "It's okay." She shrugged, clueless about the reason for his apology.

As if on cue, my pocket buzzed when the ringtone from Kai's phone chimed. I furrowed my brow and dug into my pocket. The screen lit up with the neutral colors of my ovulation tracking app. It displayed a calendar that showed exactly how many days it was until my body would be ready to try conceiving again. I swiped up to close the app. The clock that appeared on the screen reminded me to check how much time the game had left before the corruption fully overrode the system.

6:02 pm. Time had run out.

"Ebenezer Scrooge!" In the privacy of my head, I released a string of more egregious curses. I should have dived back into Fortress Clash and checked the game's clock to see if it aligned with mine, but my body froze in place. Johnson's threat, the sudden portal, and my ultimate failure to free Carlo from the game overwhelmed me to the point of numbness.

Kai had taken Wendy into his lap while he spoke in clipped sentences to the unknown voice on the phone. Worry creased his face with lines between his brow and a pull at his lips. He glanced at me as he thanked the person on the other line. His arm fell limp as he clicked to end the call.

The look in his eyes shocked me out of numbness and plagued me with all the bad feelings. Kai frowned and slowly shook his head.

"Um—" he started, then paused and covered Wendy's ears with his hands. "That was the hospital. The doctors have declared Carlo braindead."

I was here, on Earth, in my living room, surrounded by family and loved ones, but it felt like the pressure chamber as breath escaped me.

"Sora has given them the go-ahead to pull the plug when they feel it's appropriate."

"How long?" I managed to speak.

"Tomorrow morning."

Scarlet's eyes darted between us, frantic and desperate to understand. "What does that mean?"

Kai licked his lips and sighed. "He'll die."

Pain culminated into a burst of anger. Scar screamed a low-pitch, frustrated roar as she grabbed Kai's headset off the table and threw it as hard as she could. My skin prickled with goosebumps as I watched the equipment slam against the wall where Johnson had stood and it crashed to the floor.

The outburst left Wendy wailing with shock. Fat tears rolled down her reddened cheeks and I could have sworn a blanket of green surrounded her. My heart constricted with a thought that my brain refused to acknowledge fully. Though Kai squeezed her in a big hug, I rushed to her side and dropped to my knees.

Kai wiped her tears away with his thumb. And the only thing that could pull our attention from our daughter was Scarlet. She stormed across the room and yanked the front door open until it slammed against the wall behind it. Stomping footsteps faded as she vanished down the hallway.

Kai and I exchanged glances over Wendy's head where her pigtails stuck to the rough overgrowth on his chin.

With shaking hands, I touched the screen on my phone. The messages app pulled up, and I tapped Scarlet's name but skipped typing a message. I'd had enough of waiting for technology and selected to call her. The other line rang several times before it defaulted to her answering machine. It happened when I tried again, so I shot a quick message.

Where did you go?

I rubbed my temples while I waited for a response. "I'm still going to fix the game."

"No. Mari."

"What if it jump-starts Carlo's brain activity?" I stood.

"And what if Johnson comes back here?"

I felt for the strings of the hood. "That's why I have to go into the game with my real body. He came here because he couldn't access the hood on the other side. This is what he wants and I think he was trying to trick me into staying in the game so he could walk up and take the hood off of me. If I create a portal from the real world to the game, he'll follow me back to the tea party. But I need story aura—"

I glanced at Wendy. *No...* Had a fairy tale chosen her? Was that the glow I'd seen? If the gods Johnson had mentioned existed, I'd beg them to spare her. I'd pray and do their bidding and worship them if they could alter the story cycle. The way he'd spoken of them, it seemed possible, but I knew nothing about them. Was it simply the ramblings of a man one peanut short of a trail mix?

I knelt beside my family and cupped Wendy's chubby cheeks in my hands. "Mommy has to be right back, okay? Daddy will give you lots of warm hugs." I pressed my lips against her forehead and let go.

"Mari..."

I marched into the bedroom and dug for the small pistol I'd locked away for emergencies. In case Johnson got in my way again, I'd be ready to deal with him. If nothing else, I was determined to protect myself. My family needed me—my whole, complete family.

I shook my head to rid myself of thoughts of pregnancy and another baby. The situation demanded my undivided attention. When I emerged from the bedroom, Kai trailed me with his gaze as I headed to the front door to check the hall for Scarlet.

After shutting the door, I turned. I gnawed on my cheek and stared at two of the three most important people in my life.

"I know," Kai said. It was my response when he'd told me it would be okay.

Will it?

"Mari." Kai interrupted me as I started to spin away. I froze and met his gaze, expecting him to tell me to be careful. "Check for error displays or a flash drive. Corruption can look like a file that doesn't open or one that does but is unreadable. Maybe differences in the game can give you the answer like you solved with the Cheshire dragon."

I nodded and faced the wall where both Johnson and Scarlet had produced a portal. With a little help from me, the glow of magic appeared. My heart thumped at the fact that it'd worked. Under my finger, the shape of a door formed on the wall. I didn't picture Johnson's rural area of escape, but kept a clear image of the Mad Hatter's tea party in my mind.

Because of Pinocchio's aura and the story magic of something else, the two places pulled together and connected. Wherever the other aura came from, I didn't want to think about it. I'd already mistaken my daughter as the focus of *Little Red Riding Hood* when it was me. Since I was wrong last time, I wouldn't waste the energy worrying about it this time.

The portal swirled and cast the glow of bright colors from the tea party into our living room. The table full of scones and cupcakes stayed in the corner of my eye as I stared ahead at the access port.

Alice stood in her frozen position with one hand on the leaves of the bush and the other presenting her book. Instead of pages full of her adventures, the Escape button blinked.

When I stepped through, nothing pushed against me. I put one foot in front of the other. The space felt twice as small without the pressure. What once felt like a hike from the table to Alice now looked only a couple of steps away.

A slight, sweet-smelling breeze lifted the hood from the back of my legs as I took another step. Outside of the clearing, everything had been erased. The bubble of the place between portals remained the same, but the game around it was covered in complete darkness. It cast an unsettling shadow over the tea party like a massive rain cloud.

From the corner of my eye, a dark silhouette approached me.

"You're joining me," Johnson said. A cruel smile tugged at his mouth. "Good choice, leaving them." He nodded at the portal I'd created.

I spun around to see my little family framed in the shape of the magical doorway, the connection between worlds. Fear pinched Kai's face and his Adam's Apple bobbed with a heavy swallow. Slowly, he stood and set Wendy on the chair.

"What does that mean?" Though my husband was a reality away, I could hear his voice loud and clear and the strain in it broke a piece of my heart off. He couldn't possibly believe what Johnson had said was true.

I shook my head.

"You don't need them." Johnson's presence moved closer to me and brought an uncomfortable heat with it. The tickle of his breath on the back of my neck sent a shudder through my body.

I narrowed my eyes and turned. The proximity of his face might have meant to intimidate me, but I refused to give him the satisfaction of stepping back. "I'm not leaving them."

A puff of hot breath blew against me as he laughed. "You can't go back now. You're in my world now."

The pieces of Wonderland slowly darkened. The grass beneath our feet dried before our eyes, turning yellow as it died. Cupcakes sunk in on themselves and the rest of the food grew mold or rotted from the inside out.

We were officially in the game of Fortress Clash—the corruption Johnson had created. He laid his heavy hand on my shoulder and curled his fingers around the fabric of the hood.

"Mari!" Kai screamed and lunged forward in long, swooping strides. But even after all his practice of running in Pioneer Park, he wasn't fast enough. Wendy's face pinched and shaded pink again.

My voice caught in my throat as the portal to my living room rapidly shrunk smaller and smaller. I pulled from Johnson's grasp and reached for my family. If what he'd said was true, I could be separated from the only part of my life that mattered.

Though it was only two steps away, I was too late. The portal sealed, and I stumbled forward with nothing and no one to catch me as I fell. My knees slammed against the ground and the rough, thick plant life tore through my jeans. I no longer wore the character's dress from the game since I'd come here as myself.

Where my living room had been, the darkness expanded to reveal the bloody and violent world of Fortress Clash. The castle appeared in the distance beyond a forest of trees and the character's bodies lay strewn across the field where it seemed a war had taken place.

The echo of Wendy's cries was the last piece of my connection to them, but even that faded quickly. I hurried to call forth the magic and create another portal, but something blocked my access. I'd stepped into Johnson's trap, where he had complete control.

A raspy, rough voice sent a chill down my spine. "Together, we can end the stories the way the gods intended," Johnson said.

My blood boiled. I didn't know who the gods were, and I didn't care. I might have accepted the conflict in stories and that not everything would always have a perfect ending—like Mr. Darcy and Elizabeth's broken marriage and the Ugly Duckling's suicide, but it sounded like these psychotic gods expected innocent people to sacrifice their lives for the sake of the plot.

A shadow from Johnson's body cast over me as he approached. "You'll be stronger without them."

"What about Pinocchio?" I asked, without giving him the satisfaction of turning around. "You corrupted and killed him. If these gods—"

"The brothers Grimm," he corrected.

"If they want the stories to play out with the original plot lines, then you royally messed up, because the blue fairy saves Pinocchio."

Johnson scoffed. "One casualty in the pursuit of perfection is of no consequence." His vocabulary and manner of speaking had evolved here. "The gods will forgive me for trying my best." He no longer spoke in clipped sentences, and the smell of cigarettes and leather was gone. It was all an act, a persona he'd taken on, likely to fit into the real world. "I needed Pinocchio to get you here and for that, I know the brothers Grimm will smile down upon me."

I let my eyelids fall as realization flooded me. Johnson had lured me here. The hood led me to Pinocchio, and he knew it. He knew I'd chase after the story aura to help Carlo, but he'd needed me under his control—inside the game.

The car accident in San Francisco was all a stunt to attract the stupid little Keeper, and I'd fallen for it. I hung my head, the weight of my failure straining against my neck. Or was that the pull of the hood?

"Can't you at least have the decency to restore Alice? For Carlo's sake?"

"And lose this wonderful place I've created?" he laughed. "Not until I get that cloak. Then will I pull the drive out? Hmm." Johnson hummed as if considering this carefully. "I suppose it wouldn't hurt, but I doubt the fairy can save the puppet now."

My options were to confirm Carlo's death or let Johnson complete the dark fairy tales that would kill hundreds of innocent people. One life, or many? Neither sat right with me. I was the Keeper who twisted things, who'd always find a third option that Scarlet and Johnson and these supposed gods couldn't see. If a third option didn't exist right here, right now, I'd make one.

The crunch of dried grass under Johnson's boots was right behind me now. I reached into my own boot and wrapped my fingers around the pistol's cool steel handle. Johnson's hand gripped the fabric of the hood, but I willed the strings to hold firm.

I pulled from his hold for the second time, straightened, and spun around. With determination keeping my expression as a poker face, I marched straight at Johnson. He opened his hand to receive the hood, or cloak as he called it but I didn't stop.

With a cock of the pistol, I revealed the weapon from beneath the hood and I aimed between Johnson's eyes.

A laugh bubbled from his chest and spilled out of his mouth, bringing with it a wheezing cough. Maybe the icky exterior wasn't an act. I frowned and wanted to scrub the hood where his sweaty hand had grabbed with dirt-encrusted fingernails.

"You can't kill me!" he opened his arms and then patted his chest, beckoning me to shoot. A massive grin spread across his face that might have matched that of the Cheshire dragon if his teeth weren't so yellow. "I don't die."

The access port was the only aspect of Carlo's game that had remained the same, untouched by Johnson's corrupted file—no, *flash drive*. He'd called it a drive, which meant somewhere on the Access Location In Computer Enterprise was a tiny storage device full of code to override Carlo's consciousness.

"Back up," I demanded.

Johnson didn't move. "You're mad if you think you can hurt me." He laughed. "Isn't that what the Cheshire cat says? The gods know I've heard enough of these Wonderland lines."

I squinted and focused on the tangible embodiment of artificial intelligence. My gaze trailed over the blonde hair that cascaded over her blue dress.

The corruption came from something real, *something I can shoot at.* If I concentrated and aimed carefully, that was. Alice's programmed pattern repeated with the slight turn of her head over and over again. I'd spent so much time messing with the keyboard and screen inside the access port's book that I hadn't noticed the small piece of plastic that protruded from the back of her head.

"If I've gone mad, it's because you made me that way," I said.

"I did nothing." He shrugged.

"You closed my portal. And you know what?" I jabbed the barrel of the gun into his shoulder. The leather jacket crinkled under the weapon's poke. "Do you know what mad really is? It's a mama who's separated from her child."

The threat didn't affect him, as evident by the unwavering smirk on his bristly face. "So shoot me. Get your anger out so we can move on from this. It's getting dull."

I flexed my arm and straightened, aiming the gun at him, pretending to take him up on the offer. Instead, I shifted ever-so-slightly and pointed at Alice's head.

I didn't kill characters, not since the wolf had swallowed me whole. I'd sliced my way out of his stomach to save my own life, but could I bring myself to murder a gentle and innocent character? Alice was only a child, a curious girl who fell into Wonderland for adventures in the arbitrary.

But this wasn't Wonderland.

And she's not Alice. Just shoot.

Johnson lost interest in taunting me to fire at him. He grabbed for the hood—*my* hood—but I released a breath to help me focus, and aimed for the flash drive in Alice's skull.

"If you fight me, I'll just kill you," he growled.

"Go ahead, a mama is always willing to risk her life to get back to her child, and to save someone else's child." *I haven't forgotten about you, Sora.*

Though I didn't need to hold my breath at the tea party anymore, my lungs froze. The moment of all-encompassing stillness helped me aim. I pulled the trigger, and the weapon kicked back. A second later, the drive shattered, splitting into a dozen pieces of plastic.

Starting from the source, the darkness receded. Slowly but steadily, the thin, raking fingers of the corruption's shadow crawled back away from Alice's feet. The grass was full of life again, spongy and green, while rotten food with buzzing flies transformed into delicious desserts and gentle butterflies. Bright colors flooded everything and erased Johnson's creation.

With every inch of Fortress Clash that disappeared, hope swelled within me and the weight of the game's gloom lifted. The place between portals shifted and the purgatory plane seemed to unravel as the white iron gates that surrounded the clearing sagged and dripped like melting candles. They liquefied into a murky puddle that the grass absorbed.

An NPC of the White Rabbit appeared beside the table. The health bar and name above his head confirmed his status within the game. In his paw, he held a stopwatch that accurately matched Lewis Carroll's original story, but it didn't tell time.

The White Rabbit's greeting matched the same greeting I'd heard when Mr. Geppetto first logged into Fortress Clash back when the corruption had changed things.

"Now that you have joined, you are among us. We're all mad here. Welcome to Wonderland." The White Rabbit's voice sounded familiar —just like Carlo's.

Chapter 18

Black Out

Colorful surroundings, whimsical NPCs, and the bright blue sky represented Johnson's loss of control. This world wasn't Fortress Clash anymore. What his corruption had tried to erase reversed, and I clung to the hope that it'd helped Carlo.

A familiar cry echoed from somewhere beyond the happiness of the game.

A temperate breeze carried white fluff through the air that looked like pollen from California's poplar trees. Here in Wonderland, was it fairy dust? The keyboard on Alice's book lit up, and the blinking glow of the Escape key spread to every button. The screen displayed a message I hadn't seen before.

The Fairy with Azure Hair returns
fifty pennies to her dear Pinocchio
with many thanks for his kind heart

Could it mean I saved Carlo? The silent celebration within me didn't last. The shock of the gunshot wore off, and two thick hands grabbed at my shoulders. I yelped and stumbled back, losing my balance in the spongy, slick grass. I'd been so distracted by the change in the game that I'd let my guard down and Johnson got the jump on me.

The strange cry echoed again.

Dirty fingernails dug into the soft spot between my collarbone and shoulder. He yanked at the hood as I willed it to hold firm. My body went with him and the jerking motion knocked the gun from my hand. The bow tightened, but Johnson had power, the same and as strong as mine. When he gripped the smooth fabric, it pulled so hard that the tie slipped up to my neck and constricted my throat. Red thread dug into my flesh as I gasped for breath, trying to suck oxygen through my shrinking, smashed airways.

"Let it go." Cigarette breath blew into my face and soured my stomach. "Give me the damn cloak or I'll strangle you."

I wanted to spit his words back into his face. *I can't die!*

What I didn't say was spelled out with my expression. The choking hurt, but I raised my eyebrows to exert authority over him and shift the dynamic of power.

Johnson wrenched the hood tighter against my throat and a gurgling sound squelched from within me. I reached for air, desperately sucking small amounts through what felt like crushed straws.

"You think I can't kill you?" He laughed, but it was awkward and unsure. "The hood keeps you alive because its destiny is to guide the wearer to the stories. But I'm the hunter and I never stop until I finish the hunt. I can kill anything."

Tears of exertion slipped down my temples and pooled in my ears. The tie bit into my neck with such force I wondered if I'd bled. It held fast, never unraveling or fraying because it obeyed my will. I kicked and pulled and pushed against Johnson, but the lack of air left me with little energy and he overpowered me.

The cry filled the surrounding air in a voice I recognized. It pricked my heart and sent my sensations into overdrive. The sudden need to run to Wendy's bedroom overwhelmed me as it often would when she'd cry like a baby and it would wake me from my dreams.

Johnson wrenched the hood tighter and a ring of darkness seeped into my vision.

Kai was right all along. He'd smelled the threat to my life coming from a mile—or a virtual world—away. And just as I always did, I'd failed to listen. I couldn't accept the truth and now my reality was death by strangling under the hand of the man who'd come from The Little Cloak Girl's story. Who was I to think I could fight four hundred years of culminated strength and power?

I'd officially lost all control, and I could do nothing but accept it.

Not all stories have happy endings.

Thoughts faded, and my vision darkened. Chills ran up my arms and everything felt icy, which created dissonance with the temperate world of Wonderland. Like Alice, my oxygen-deprived brain struggled to break beyond a repetition of words.

Not all stories have happy endings.

I squeezed my eyes shut and used the last bit of awareness I had left to snap from the cyclical thought. The stopwatch in the White Rabbit's paw didn't tick because time in the Mad Hatter's tea party didn't exist. I'd die in the space between time because no amount of kicking and flailing deterred Johnson.

Except Wonderland didn't exist either, not beyond the virtual plane created by Carlo. Scarlet had sealed Alice's story long before we'd met, and the portals that kept the space between the fictional world and the real world alive had closed. So, where were we if not inside the game?

The realization clued me into the surroundings. Wonderland had melted away like the iron gates that spilled into milky puddles and dried up. Now we existed, just me and Johnson in a plane of colorlessness.

The cry continued, except this time it came with a word. The sounds of the letters jumbled in my mind like a jigsaw puzzle.

"Let go, Mari," Johnson grunted.

I closed my eyes and drowned out his demand. When I focused on the familiar voice and the one-word cry, it became clearer.

Mommy!

I pictured our living room, calling forth the story aura that existed there. I'd never wanted to return to reality so badly. Once I made it home, I'd never look back or run away and hide in the escape of a video game or book. These things were meant to entertain, relieve stress, and be enjoyed in a healthy way. But I'd used them to pretend the crap in my life didn't exist rather than face the truth.

I reached out my hand to confirm where I was. Instead of the fairy dust in Wonderland, my fingers brushed something solid, wooden, the frame of a doorway. The last portal was mine, and we stood on the threshold. All I had to do was gather enough strength to step into my living room.

Johnson wrenched me back and breathed another demand to give up the cloak. Instead of fighting back and kicking at him, I extended my leg and used the last bit of energy I had to pull forward.

When I stepped forward, a warm hand grabbed mine and laced our fingers in an unbreakable weave. But the pull between the new force and Johnson's strength threatened to tear me apart. The hunter still had his hold on the hood and the tie cut off all the air now. I flexed every muscle in my limbs and torso, refusing to give either force a win over my body.

"It's okay," my husband's voice registered somewhere in my consciousness as darkness overcame me.

I'd accepted my reality as the Keeper and clung to the hood I'd wanted to throw away. This was my story and I could choose any ending I wanted, just like I'd twisted Red Riding Hood's plot.

And I chose the opposite ending of The Little Cloak Girl. Unlike her parents, I'd return to my daughter no matter what it took to get there, but I needed to accept the help my husband had tried to give me all along.

I stopped resisting and let Kai pull me through.

Before I fainted, I recognized the coffee table, and couch, and Wendy's pinched, reddened face.

I was home.

Chapter 19

Changing Tunes

The moment of unconsciousness ended with an abrupt gasp. My eyes shot open to see only seconds had passed. I'd collapsed on the rug on our living room floor and two men stood at my feet.

The muscles in Kai's forearms strained and flexed as he used every bit of strength to shove Johnson back into the frame of the portal. The glow around the doorway receded, swallowing the hunter inside.

"The brothers are coming for you!" Johnson shouted. "The gods will destroy you." His voice dulled and muffled as the portal sealed and the wall returned to a plain, poorly painted load-bearing structure that held our house together.

Old crayon marks and dirty fingerprints marred the wall, but the entrance to the place between portals left no trace of its existence. A weight descended on me as a little body climbed onto my stomach.

Wendy laced her arms around my neck and dropped her head against the soft spot next to my collarbone. I winced from the pressure on my bruised skin, but ignored it. Johnson may have left a mark, but I didn't need to let it ruin my daughter's hug.

I lifted my arms and wrapped her up, burying my nose in the mess of her pigtails. With Kai's help, I sat up and scooted back to lean against the back of the side chair. He dropped to his knees next to me and took both of us in one of his famous warm Olaf hugs.

Bliss temporarily dulled the throbbing injuries throughout my body. I relished the moment of pure relief and joy that only comes when I'm fully present with my family or when I solved an investigation or wrote an article that helped keep someone safe.

But something was missing, and a hollow sadness sparked my heartbeat to pick up the pace.

My phone buzzed from deep inside my pocket, so I shifted to the side to tug it out. Scarlet's face covered the screen with a silly memory of her on Halloween last year. The three of us had taken Wendy on a walk through the city where she knocked on doors and presented her basket per trick-or-treat tradition. Scarlet had dressed up as her favorite villain from The Lion King and I'd set the picture as her contact tag. The memory made me smile, shifting the empty space inside me as my heartache faded.

"You talk to her while I grab the first aid kit," Kai said as he stood.

I swiped right and brought the speaker to my ear.

"I'm going to make you an offer you can't refuse," she said. I burst into a short laugh at the absurdity of Scarlet's greeting as a movie quote.

"What's that?"

"If you leave right now and bring a headset to the hospital, I'll babysit Wendy for free whenever you want."

I straightened, and Wendy looked up from her snuggled place in my lap. "Is Carlo okay?" I asked.

"Mari, it's bad. His body is normal again, and the wooden limbs are completely gone. There's still no brain activity, even though he's not a puppet anymore." Emotion wracked her voice. "The story is over and Pinocchio is fixed, but the doctors don't see it that way. They're going to let him die!"

With the plot completed, the story aura would have vanished, leaving Carlo vulnerable to death. The blue fairy had done her job. Now it was up to us to stop the doctors from pulling the plug.

I glanced at the headset left on the Coffee Table of Evidence and wished for more energy. If only I had a fairy of my own to grant me strength. But I didn't, so a half-empty first aid kit and caffeine would have to do.

Kai agreed to pour a cup of cold brew into a water bottle only after he rubbed cooling lotion over the crimson line on my neck. Where the strings had dug into me, the skin burned. Armed with a bottle full of coffee and a headset, Kai followed me out of the house. I secured Wendy in her car seat and climbed into the backseat.

Kai acted as our chauffeur, just as he'd done when we first drove Wendy home from the hospital. I didn't miss the days of worrying over my newborn's fragile life, full of screeching cries and stinky diapers. If we had a baby right now, we'd be slower—forced to grab a bag full of butt cream and booger suctioning bulbs. Not to mention I'd be physically worse off, weaker from lack of sleep, and less able to fight the injuries I suffered. What I'd once welcomed as part of parenting a newborn no longer fit into my lifestyle.

Wendy's newfound independence *was* my wish for strength granted from my own personal fairy named The Next Stage of Life. The stage that suited our family's goals and dreams and responsibilities right now. On the ride, Wendy busied herself with the first aid kit. Dozens of papers scattered the floor by the backseat as she peeled bandages and stuck them on my arms.

The car's engine switched off after Kai pulled into a tight parking spot at Golden Heart Hospital. He carried Wendy while I brought the headset. We skipped the slow-moving elevator and opted to drag our bodies up the staircase, hoping to save time. The muscles in my legs screamed at me to rest. After today, I'd collapse in my bed and sleep for as long as Wendy would let me. Of course, our vacation time ended on Tuesday and my boss expected me to return to work at Bay Side Media.

So much for sleep.

When we rounded the corner into Carlo's room, Scarlet leaped up from a chair opposite where Sora sat. His mother used both of her hands to hold his and only tilted her chin up when we entered. Grief left her features sagged and a collection of creases below her eyes.

Scar grabbed the headset and bent over Carlo's bed. With more softness than I'd ever seen in the eyes of someone whose favorite character was the villain in Lion King, Scarlet gently lifted Carlo's head and pulled the VR equipment onto his face.

Moments passed with only the rhythmic beep of Carlo's machine-powered heartbeat. Everyone held their breath in a collective gathering of hope and patience.

A small voice broke the silence, and Wendy tugged my fingers. I tore my gaze from Carlo long enough to glimpse my daughter's enormous eyes.

"I need to go potty."

Yeah, Wendy is definitely enough for our family right now.

Without a word, Kai took her hand and led her from the room. The bustle of the hall drifted into the calm of Carlo's space.

Scar, Sora, and I exchanged silent glances. With every second that passed, hope slipped away. Scarlet lifted shaking fingers to her face and covered her mouth to stifle a sob.

Sora gasped, and a tear slipped down her cheek. She lifted the hand she had cupped in her grasp. "He's squeezing back," she said. "Carlo's awake!"

Acting quickly, Scarlet put a hand on either side of the headset and lifted it. With large, dark eyes, Carlo shifted his gaze between his mother and his friend.

He didn't notice me, and I didn't mind. I took the opportunity to slip from the room and alert the nurses that Carlo needed his ventilator removed, leaving Scarlet and Sora to hold his hands. The door eased shut behind me and I made my way to the nurses' station. After passing on the message, I turned around to see Wendy bounding up to me.

Pigtails bounced as she skipped down the hallway, a cheerful sight with her bright dress and beaming smile among the sterile white of Golden Heart's walls. I returned her smile and stooped to scoop her into my arms. Everything ached and my arms threatened to snap off since she was a big girl now and getting harder to hold every day. Once again, I didn't mind.

Kai tilted his head. "Good news?"

I nodded. "Carlo's awake." The crack in my voice revealed that I no longer had the strength to hold back emotion. "It worked."

After a doctor and several nurses poured into Carlo's room, Scarlet popped out the door, trading places with them.

"Restroom," she said as she pointed at the sign down the hall. "I've been holding Carlo's hand all day and refused to let go. Now I don't want to watch the doctor-y stuff."

We watched Scar hurry to the restroom with the faintness skip in her step. When she disappeared through the door, Kai folded his arms.

"Do you ever feel like she's kind of our daughter too?" he mused.

I laughed. "Definitely."

"Can we go to McDonald's?" Wendy asked, oblivious to the profound moment between her parents. Did Kai come to the same conclusion I had about our family? "I want a Happy Meal."

"Sure," I said as we made our way to the elevator. The doors slid shut and Wendy bobbed her head, humming the McDonald's jingle on our way down.

A scratchy speaker blared an old tune and drowned out Wendy's little song. A distantly familiar lullaby drifted into the elevator. The music announced the birth of a brand new baby somewhere within the hospital—hopefully in the maternity ward if the mother had made it in time.

Wendy grabbed a chunk of my hair and started twisting it into her version of a braid. "I'm making you look like Elsa."

Sure, kid. If your imagination is good enough to picture short, black hair matching the queen of Arendelle, have at it.

"Hey, um, Kai?" I turned to him as the elevator came to a halt and dinged. "I think I'm happy with our family how it is."

His shoulder dropped, and he released a breath. "Oh, thank goodness."

"Yeah?"

"After today, I realized I can't look after another baby on top of taking care of Wendy and you." He walked out of the elevator and I followed close enough to give him a light punch in the arm with my free hand.

"Hey, I can take care of myself."

"Right. Tell that to the security guard at Everly Woods preschool."

My jaw dropped, and I shook my head at him. "Low blow."

The double doors slid open to allow us to exit into the parking lot. An ambulance flicked off his siren as it pulled into the covered round-about at the urgent care building across the lot. Clouds darkened the sky and threatened the first rain of the coming autumn season. I planned to spend the last day of the holiday weekend curled on the couch or in bed and marathoning the *Frozen* movies with Wendy. Labor Day wouldn't live up to its name for me. We'd rest and recover and be ready for the week ahead.

As soon as I snapped the buckles of Wendy's car seat together, I pulled out my phone and shot Scarlet a message.

We're headed home, but tell Carlo we said hi.

I tapped my thumb against the side of the phone and then continued typing. *Also, if you want to take the week off to hang out with him, I'll clear it with Pam and pick up your workload.*

I dropped into the passenger seat and connected with the safety belt. The buzz of Scarlet's response came with several messages that repeated her thanks. Another one popped up with *I'll be back.* I snorted. Whether Scar quoted the Terminator or it was just confirmation that she still wanted her job, I read it in the infamous cyborg assassin's voice. But it sparked another thought, a more sobering memory of someone's return.

Johnson had claimed the gods were coming for me. Who were these supposed brothers? Did they exist, or was the hunter simply one peanut short of a trail mix?

The ride to McDonald's and subsequent wait in the drive-through line gave me time to Google gods from classic myths and legends. Many of them were brothers, especially in the Greek and Roman mythologies, but only two brothers in history, legend, or myth went by the name of Grimm.

I frowned and glanced back at the miniature version of me, who happily kicked her long legs against the back of my chair. Wendy insisted Kai order the Happy Meal with her exact parameters and he obliged, always the dad who gave in to spoiling.

"Chocolate milk and apple slices," Wendy demanded.

"Are you sure you don't want french fries? You always eat my fries." Kai twisted away from the driver's open window to catch Wendy's response.

"Fries too." She nodded.

The faintest glow surrounded her, and a lump gathered in my throat. The green aura wasn't a piece of my imagination conjured by fear. It existed, obvious and clear—cementing my daughter's role in a real, live fairy tale.

Ebenezer Scrooge.

If these gods were legitimate, I'd track them down and demand they rewrite whichever story had landed on Wendy. Nobody comes between a mama and her child, not even the Brothers Grimm.

Chapter 20

Bury the Hatchet

(Tuesday)

At Everly Woods preschool, Miss Jenna greeted all the parents and caregivers who dropped off their children. Four-year-olds leaped and bounded and chatted as they found their seats among short, round tables.

After the first week of school, the classroom changed. Dozens of colorful drawings lined the walls below, hanging alphabet signs and inspirational posters with pictures of puppies and kittens. The neatly organized towers of crayons had turned into piles of waxy nubs in the center of the tables.

The children knew exactly what to do. They started the day armed with a blank sheet of paper and whichever crayon they'd grabbed first to draw the emotion they felt today.

Wendy scribbled a big smiling face on her paper and colored it green. It was just a coincidence, right? Maybe she was just feeling envious of her tablemate's full, sharpened crayon.

"Miss Hook." The tablemate raised his hand.

"Call me Miss Jenna," the teacher corrected. "What is it, Xander?"

I liked the Buffy the Vampire-inspired name, but it wasn't the boy's name that piqued my interest.

Hook? It's another coincidence. Nothing more than a coincidence.

"Can we have snack time before we draw today?" Xander whined. "I'm hungry."

"We will follow our schedule as usual," she said.

I knelt next to Wendy and gave her a quick squeeze and Déjà vu hit me like a ton of bricks when Miss Jenna appeared in front of me. Her thin nose most certainly wasn't crooked and nothing in the classroom resembled an oven. But a pirate's ship…

I stood and offered my hands up in surrender. "I was just leaving."

"No rush. The first day of school is always so stressful for kids, but admittedly it is for me too. I might have jumped to calling the security officer too quickly. It's just that if one child's parent lingers, then the other students become unruly and no amount of organization will direct their attention." Miss Jenna wrung her hands as she spoke. "I'm fairly new as a teacher, so I hope you'll forgive me for being rash last week."

Kids scribbled and colored while discussing TV shows as seriously as an adult might discuss the stock market. They traded recommendations by demanding the rest of the class to watch their favorite show.

"No worries," I said. "I've learned to let go a little since her first day. Parents can't stop their kids from getting older."

The teacher sighed and perched her hands on her hips. "Well, if it makes you feel any better, last week Wendy told me she never wants to grow up."

I wrinkled my nose, but it wasn't because of the smell of urine in the air. Miss Jenna gasped and squeaked out an 'oops' and words of reassurance as she guided little Xander to the tiny potty. She instructed him to close the door while she retrieved dry pants from his backpack.

Was it all a coincidence? The green glow, Miss Jenna's last name, and the teacher's comment about what Wendy had said?

Speaking of Miss Hook, she returned from delivering Xander's clean pants. The sting of hand sanitizer burned my nose as she rubbed her hands together.

"If you'd like to stick to the words in the book, I'd be happy to let you read the kids a story this time. They actually enjoyed your spooky version of Snow White, so I'd suggest one of the cute little ghost stories on the shelf." The teacher pointed to the alphabetized books on the shelf across the room.

The offer was sweet and unlike Peter Pan's villain. Plus, the teacher didn't have a speck of story aura on her. I refused to repeat my paranoia from last week and forced myself to smile.

Miss Jenna might not have been Captain Hook, but Wendy was definitely a fairy tale character. With a shake of my head, I turned down the teacher's offer.

I didn't have time for ghost stories. I had two gods to find by the name of Grimm.

Epilogue

Dear Journal,

I've just survived the most intense two weeks of my life. Honestly, I didn't think I could even get that emotional, but when death, infertility, and failure all build up like a stack of crayons, you get crushed under all the colors. That's a terrible metaphor. As a journalist, you'd think I'd be skilled at writing, but I'm simply too tired to be creative.

Though I spent most of my vacation standing in the middle of my living room with video game equipment on my head, it feels like I've traveled hundreds of miles to dozens of places. Portals will do that to you. Oh, yeah, I failed at a lot of junk, but I finally learned how to create portals, and then I trapped Johnson inside of one like Han Solo in Carbonite. Thankfully, the mold of the hunter's body isn't sticking out of the wall by our front door.

And thankfully (x2), Johnson told me about the bastards who just might be responsible for the story cycle and all things fictional-come-life. They're the god forms of the Brothers Grimm and, apparently, they're coming for me.

That's a good thing. I plan to meet them halfway.

If Wendy is actually her counterpart in the story of the boy who doesn't grow up, then I'll lose her to the plot's destiny. As far as I know, Peter Pan runs away and never returns.

But gods are all-powerful, right? They can change Peter's story and I won't stop fighting until they do. No fairy tale bullcrap can come between a mama and her daughter.

UP NEXT IS ANOTHER WILD, SUPERNATURAL MYSTERY FULL OF GHOSTS AND FAIRY TALES. IN THE NEXT BOOK, MARI WILL JOURNEY INTO THE NEXT STAGE OF MOTHERHOOD AND A NEW PHASE AS THE KEEPER OF STORIES WHERE SHE'LL CONFRONT GODS AND LEARN HOW THE FABRIC BETWEEN REALITY AND FICTION RIPPED OPEN.

A GRIMM HAUNTING RELEASES ON DECEMBER 5TH, 2022.

PLEASE CONSIDER LEAVING A REVIEW AT YOUR FAVORITE PLACE TO PURCHASE BOOKS IF YOU ENJOYED THIS STORY! ALSO, A SHARE WITH YOUR FRIENDS WHO LOVE CLEAN, SWEET, SMALL-TOWN ROMANCES WOULD BE GREATLY APPRECIATED. MY QUEST AS AN AUTHOR IS TO MAKE OTHERS FEEL SEEN THROUGH THE ADVENTURE OF FICTION. PLEASE REACH OUT TO ME AND LET ME KNOW IF MY STORIES HAVE TOUCHED YOU. YOU, DEAR READER, ARE WHO THIS BOOK WAS WRITTEN FOR.

About the Author

Congenital Heart Defect survivor, Emily Fluke, finds joy and peace through the expression of writing. She is a strong believer that all stories need a little magic and a lot of excitement. Emily and her husband spend their free time wrangling two children and playing video games in their busy California lifestyle. Otherwise, you'll find Emily solving an escape room, running, or writing Magic the Gathering-based poetry.

To stay up to date on new releases and connect with me, visit my website at Emilyfluke.com or follow me on social media under Author Emily Fluke, or @emilyflukefairytales